"Are you enjoying yourself?" Faye screamed.

Joe stepped out into full view. "So you think I would stoop so low to sneak about to watch you take a bath." He picked up her towel and placed it on her shoulders. "Woman, I've better things to do with my time."

She stood with her mouth agape, clutching the towel. "Why are you here? Did you come to freshen up in the creek also?"

"I could've left you here all alone, but I had to make sure you were all right."

"And while doing so you took advantage of the situation," she said, her lower lip curved in a pout. "Thank goodness I hadn't taken off all of my clothes. You would really have gotten an eyeful then, wouldn't you have?"

He leaned his face down toward hers. "It's not as though I've never seen you without your clothes on before, you know. Or do you forget all that easily?"

Dear Reader:

Harlequin offers you historical romances with a difference—novels with all the passion and excitement of a 500 page historical in 300 pages. Your letters indicate that many of you are pleased with this shorter length. Another difference is that the main focus of our stories is on people—a hero and heroine you really care about.

We have some terrific books scheduled this month and in the coming months: Cassie Edwards fans should look for *A Gentle Passion*; the second book in Heather Graham Pozzessere's trilogy, *Rides a Hero*, tells Shannon's story; *Samara* by Patricia Potter is the sequel to her award-winning *Swampfire*; Nora Roberts's *Lawless* is an unforgettable Western. You won't want to miss these and any of the other exciting selections coming from Harlequin Historicals.

Please keep your letters coming. You can write to us at the address below.

Karen Solem
Editorial Director
Harlequin Historicals
P.O. Box 7372
Grand Central Station
New York, New York 10017

A Gentle Passion

Cassie Edwards

Harlequin Books

TORONTO • NEW YORK • LONDON
AMSTERDAM • PARIS • SYDNEY • HAMBURG
STOCKHOLM • ATHENS • TOKYO • MILAN

For Tracy Farrell, my excellent, devoted
editor, who cares; for Karen Solem for
opening the doors for me at Harlequin; and
for Leslie Wainger who suggested it!

and

For Susan Feldhake, a talented author,
close friend and confidante.

Harlequin Historical first edition March 1989

ISBN 0-373-28617-1

Books by Cassie Edwards

Harlequin Historicals

Passion in the Wind #5
A Gentle Passion #17

CASSIE EDWARDS

is the author of over twenty romances and has traveled the U.S. doing research for her books. When she's not on the road, Cassie spends seven days a week writing in her office in the Illinois home she shares with her husband, Charlie.

Acknowledgments

A big thank-you goes to Janie Glover of the Fort Smith, Arkansas, Chamber of Commerce for her assistance in the research of Fort Smith.

Chapter One

The Arkansas Ozarks, rough and forbidding, stretched for as far as the eye could see. Flocks of turkeys, prairie chickens and quail flew in and out of the waist-high waving grass, and the wrinkled hills were alive with the yellow and blue of blossoming flowers. A wild and rugged beauty lured the travelers past the sandstone bluff ridgetops and through the narrow valleys with their willow-fringed streams.

Resembling a fleet of sailing ships, fifty Conestoga covered wagons ambled along, drawn by slow-moving, lumbering oxen. Their red-and-blue wagons with the white canvas tops were gay and colorful as they wound through the mountain passes.

A number of boys and men carrying rifles walked alongside the wagons, herding their cattle. Escorting the long caravan from the Arkansas and Mississippi borders to the safety of Fort Smith were members of the Fort Smith cavalry unit, resplendent in blue uniforms with shining sabers hanging from their belts.

Her long brown hair loose and flowing in the gentle breeze, Faye Poincaré walked alongside a wagon, kicking the hem of her full-skirted gingham dress away from her feet. Carrying a rifle, she defied anyone to get in her way, having begun to understand the courage that was required to survive now that she no longer had parents to depend on. A tragic riverboat accident just north of New Orleans had taken the lives of her parents, and now Faye was on her way to live with her brother, Michael, a priest at a mission established close to Fort Smith.

At the time that she had managed to make arrangements to travel to Arkansas from New Orleans with Celia and Gayland Johnston, Faye had known that this journey through the wilderness would not be easy. But Michael was all the kin that she had left, and it was Michael's duty to see to it that she was cared for. So overwhelmed had she been by her parents' death that Faye could think only of reaching her brother. After relinquishing a portion of her inheritance to the Johnstons to cover the travel expenses, she had turned her back on the refinements of New Orleans and with a brave heart marched toward the rough and primitive outpost.

Faye now understood why her parents had tried to persuade her to marry any of a number of gentlemen who had escorted her to the fancy balls in New Orleans. The elder Poincarés had wanted her taken care of in case anything happened to them.

Blithely she had ignored their promptings, for she had felt nothing special for any of the men. She had found them all stuffy and boring, and she had wanted the freedom of the right to choose a man when she saw fit, when she was ready.

Even now at age eighteen she wanted this freedom of choice, but what sort of men would there be to choose from in this dreaded, isolated wilderness? Most men traveling with this procession were with their wives and children. Gazing ahead, she looked at the soldiers, so stiff atop their horses.

Then she looked at Bart Dobbs and Joe Harrison, two scouts who had begun escorting the wagon train as soon as it had reached the Arkansas border. Seemingly in full command, they led the wagons along Indian trails and animal paths and across rivers.

Faye studied Bart Dobbs as he lumbered along on his Appaloosa. He was a jovial enough man, even kind, but his stooped shoulders, red hair and side whiskers hardly appealed to Faye. His leathery, freckled face was so weathered and wrinkled from years of being exposed to the sun that she would be hard pressed to guess his age.

Her gaze shifted to Joe Harrison, who traveled on a handsome brown mare in a fancy hand-tooled saddle with a silver horn and mountings. The sight of his lean, rugged frame atop the horse thrilled her in a way she did not want to acknowledge even to herself. He looked younger than Bart, perhaps in his late twenties, and his shoulder-length hair was so black it appeared blue in the bright sunlight.

Joe Harrison had a Roman nose and coal black eyes, and his skin had been bronzed by the sun. He wore a loose deerskin shirt open at the throat to reveal a mat of dark hair. A powder horn, sheath knife and bullet pouch hung from leather thongs over his shoulder. A *dague*, a broad, double-edged knife used to cut up the carcass of the buffalo, was tucked into the heavy leather belt at his waist. Suddenly the holstered revolvers hanging low about his hips caught her eye. Faye gasped faintly, her gaze flickering back to Joe Harrison's face. Yes, if need be, he was prepared to draw.

There was no doubt how this man stirred Faye's desire. Frowning darkly, she turned to look straight ahead. Intriguing or unforgettable, he was arrogant and wild and purposefully annoying. He seemed to take great pleasure in interfering in her life and bossing her around!

Angry with herself, Faye walked determinedly onward, feeling empty inside over what life had handed her. She missed her parents desperately! She missed the life that she had been forced to leave behind. In the wilderness she would have no social life whatsoever. She loved to dress up in fancy gowns and attend elaborate balls. She had enjoyed the attention of the men. She was used to the comforts of life—personal maids, fresh linens and French perfumes.

Thinking about what life had in store for her now sent her into abject misery. Everything was such an incredible change for her. How was she ever to adjust to life in a mission?

"Indeed, if I ever arrive there," she whispered to herself, shooing a buzzing fly with her free hand. Every day the journey's trials seemed to get worse. This morning, to give Celia and Gayland a moment of privacy, she felt forced to walk instead of ride. The gun was heavy in her tired hand, but she dared not walk without it. The tall grass hid many dangers along the trail.

At the thought, her gaze moved back to Joe Harrison. He might prove to be her largest threat of all. Angrily, she placed one foot in front of the other, determined to keep pace.

Sharp briars clung to the skirt of her dress. Using the muzzle of her rifle, Faye tried to brush the annoying briars aside, only to have several pierce the skirt and become imbedded in the soft material of her stockings. Wincing, she stopped and leaned down to try to free herself of the sharp, sticky prick-ers.

She gave the wagon occasional nervous glances as it ambled on away from her. The Johnston wagon was the last in the procession of many, and Faye did not feel safe lagging behind. Tales of wolves, moun-tain lions and Indians were told over and over again, and the danger was very real. Even now the caravan was being watched by several Osage hunting par-ties—roving buffalo hunters who thus far had posed no true threat to the newest settlers arriving in Ar-kansas. But to Faye, their presence helped to keep her nervous and frightened.

Clumsily dropping her rifle to the ground, she pulled at her skirt. The thorny briars hopelessly imbedded, she cursed colorfully in her native French.

"Oh, la vache!" she murmured, her gaze follow-ing the wagon as it moved farther away from her. Attempting to take a few steps in the matted wheel tracks, she swore again, this time loudly. Blood surged to her cheeks when she realized that Joe Har-rison had broken rank and was quickly riding to-ward her. If it could be anyone but him, she thought to herself desperately.

"Now that wasn't a very ladylike thing to say," the scout said, reining in beside Faye.

His deep, resonant voice caused Faye's pulse to quicken. As she turned her eyes slowly to him, an unwanted thrill swept through her. He was handsome, but it was not his looks that set her on edge. It was his arrogance, the very thing that rankled her nerves, that made him intriguing and exciting. Even now she could see a glint of mockery in his dark eyes as he sat smugly in his saddle, peering down at her.

Annoyed by a slow smile lifting his lips, Faye felt her cheeks grow hotter. Though she had not suspected that he was of French descent, she should have realized that he would know the language. He seemed to know everything and would never allow her to forget it.

Looking ahead at the wagons moving on away from her, Faye began to feel desperate. She gave Joe an annoying stare. "You're enjoying this, aren't you, *monsieur*?" she said icily. "I'm sure you just watch and wait for me to look foolish and clumsy."

Joe lifted one shoulder in a gesture of indifference. "Ma'am, can I help it if that seems to be at every turn of the trail?" he teased, chuckling. His horse snorted and dipped its nose into the grass, and the saddle leather groaned as he leaned his face down closer to Faye's. "Now wouldn't it be best if you just rode in the wagon? That's where most women stay, you know."

Joe raked his gaze over her, troubled by how she affected him. He had lost at love once and vowed it would never happen again. Now this French girl's lustrous and sparkling yet impudent blue eyes looked up at him, challenging his every word and movement.

But it wasn't only her eyes that he found disturbing. She had a full, ripe mouth, a sublime, long neck, and creamy skin. Her face was young and sweet, framed by long, billowing brown hair, and though the dress that she wore did not reveal much to the naked eye with its crisp white collar hugging her neck, nothing could hide the fact that she was supple and slender with a small waist and high, rounded breasts.

Everything about her stirred something primitive in Joe, yet he did not trust his feelings any more than he would ever trust her, or any other woman for that matter. Since Kathryn Quincy had claimed to love him then left him, he could not find it easy ever to trust again.

"Riding in the wagon is the only way a helpless woman should travel, I might add," Joe said purposely to torment her. "Your sort sure can get into a peck of trouble."

Faye's spine stiffened as she glared up at him. He had finally said what he had silently implied for so long. He did see her as helpless, clumsy and more than likely downright foolish.

He had some nerve, she thought to herself angrily. She would show him. Somehow she would prove to him just how wrong he was. Stooping and picking up her rifle, she began a slow boil inside as he continued to banter with her.

"And ain't it just like a lady?" Joe said, his eyes dancing. "You're more worried about your dress than your own welfare."

He nodded toward the departing wagons. "It's going to take some mighty good running on your part to catch up, don't you think?"

Faye placed her free hand on her hip, her eyes flashing. "*Monsieur*, that's not your concern," she snapped, not letting him know just how bothered she was at being left behind, especially with him. "And even if it were, you should go on your way and quit disturbing me so that I could catch up."

Joe circled his large hands around the pommel of his saddle and leaned forward. He smiled amusedly down at Faye. "Lady, I'm not stopping you," he said in a drawl. "You're the one who seems always to enjoy bantering with me." He gestured with a hand. "Take off running. I won't stop you."

Faye breathed hard, her anger almost uncontrollable. "*I* enjoy bantering with *you*?" she cried. "You are insulting!"

Abruptly, his horse blew out a snort, shook its mane and pawed nervously at the ground. Faye's eyes wavered when she saw a look of sudden alarm in Joe's dark eyes as he looked past her, over her shoulder.

She was taken completely off guard as Joe swept a powerful arm down and thrust it about her waist. Shocked by his audacity, she kicked wildly in an effort to free herself, only to find her blind anger replaced by a searing humiliation as her skirt ripped up to her thigh. Having been yanked from the ground, she was in the uncomfortable position of being held steady on Joe's lap while he snapped his horse's reins and rode briskly away with her.

In vain she attempted to keep her balance, hold on to the rifle and cover her bare calves. When she finally was able to collect her senses, she clamped her fingers onto Joe's arm and tried to remove it from around her waist. "*Que faites-vous?* Let me go," she stormed. "Let me down! I need not be transported back to the wagon. *Oh, la vache!* Let me down. I can walk!"

"Tsk, tsk," Joe admonished, holding tight as he rode on toward the wagon train. "You are a spitfire, aren't you? Where did you learn such language?"

"Where did you learn French?" she said, eyeing him hotly. "It is apparent that you are hardly more than a savage."

Joe's eyes narrowed angrily. "Ma'am, one doesn't have to be French to speak French," he said sourly. "And one doesn't have to attend the finest schools to learn the language. Being the savage that I am, I got my education from others just like me."

Faye was stung by Joe's angry coldness. "Why are you doing this?" she asked in a more gentle tone.

"I could have left you there to be snakebit," Joe taunted. "But I don't think that would have been too pleasant, do you?"

Faye paled and looked past his shoulder. "A snake was there, so close to me?" she gasped. "Why didn't you shoot it?"

"Snakes have a purpose in life just the same as you and I," Joe said, his insides aflame with the feel of her ripe curves pressed so intimately against him.

"*Oui*, like biting poor innocent folk like myself," Faye said sarcastically.

"Only because you were in its way," Joe argued. "Snakes fight for survival the same as man. Can't blame them, now can we?"

Knowing she could never best him, Faye tired of the bantering. Soon, though, she wished she was still listening to his arrogant lecturing. At least when he talked, she couldn't hear the steady, strong beat of his heart or the sound of his breathing as he pulled the air deep into his lungs. The close confines of his lap made her achingly aware of him as a man, not that she had never thought of him in this way before.

Though she had fought it, he had filled her midnight dreams these past several nights since she'd first seen him. In her dreams, his arms had felt as wonderful and as comforting as they did now. His muscles had been as corded and as powerful, his smell of worn leather and fresh, clean soap as heavenly.

But she could not allow these feelings to take over. Arrogance in a man was something that she did not know how to cope with. He was a man who seemed not to want a woman's presence in his life. Nor would she want his in hers.

Her relief at the approach of Gayland's wagon was short-lived as Joe crudely lifted her from his lap and placed her on the seat beside Gayland Johnston, whose pale gray eyes widened with shock to see her deposited there in such a way.

"Gayland, I'd suggest you keep a better eye on your passenger, or she just may never make it to Fort Smith," Joe said, glowering down at Faye as she positioned herself more comfortably on the seat. He gave her a lingering stare, then spurred his brown mare in a gallop away from her.

"Faye? What on earth did Joe Harrison mean?" Gayland asked, his balding head peeling from a sunburn. With his free hand, he smoothed the beads of sweat from his brow, wiping his palm on his dark, denim breeches. "I thought you were walking beside the wagon. Where did you go?"

Her heart still pounding, Faye shook her thick mane of hair away from her face.

Holding up her ripped dress so that Gayland could see the tear, she laughed awkwardly. "It seems that

I got tangled up in some briars,'' she said, her voice apologetic. "That led me to more entanglements. Joe Harrison. It seems that he's always close by." She bit her lower lip in frustration. "That man irritates me so!'' she said in a huff.

"What were you doing on his horse with him?'' Gayland persisted, snapping the whip against the oxen's backs.

"Gayland, if Joe hadn't sidetracked me, it wouldn't have been necessary for him to carry me back,'' she said, trying to convince herself of her story. "The fact that I was returned here is all that matters. Please, let's not discuss it anymore.''

She looked over her shoulder. "Where's Celia?'' she murmured. "Is she taking another nap?''

"Yes,'' Gayland said, frowning. "Perhaps leaving New Orleans was a bad decision. Celia isn't bearing up at all well under the hardships of travel. She's so tiny and frail. If not for the lure of free land, I never would have attempted this again. Traveling from Kentucky to New Orleans twenty years ago was easier. Celia and I were much younger in those days.''

Faye patted Gayland's arm reassuringly. "Neither of you looks anywhere near your age, and don't worry about Celia. She'll do just fine,'' she said. Yet at the same time she wondered even about herself. How on earth would she ever make it? Thus far, it had been hard, and it surely was not going to get easier. "I don't know how I'll ever be able to thank you for adding me to your burdens of travel."

"It's been my pleasure, Faye," Gayland said, again snapping the whip against the oxen's backs. "It's been good for Celia, being childless and all. You've become important to her, but I guess you know that."

"I'm glad she and I have become such good friends," Faye said, smiling at him. "I feared that I would be nothing more than extra baggage for you in such close quarters as these."

"We look to you as family," Gayland said, patting Faye's arm. He nodded toward the wagon. "Go on. Go make yourself comfortable. It won't be long till we'll be making camp. You won't have any time for rest once you start preparing the meal."

"*Oui, merci*, I believe I will go inside," Faye said, eager to rid herself of the sight of Joe Harrison's back as he rode not more than four or five paces ahead of them. Her recent experience had shaken her more than she would dare to let on to anyone. "I'll see to Celia."

As the afternoon became evening, deep purples and grays shaded the distant hills. The sun was a pale red, casting its last rays across a landscape of bronze and green. A chill wind blew through the grass, and in the dim pewter light the cottonwoods spread their long shadows along a nearby creek.

Gayland eyed the setting sun and gave Faye a troubled glance. "Back home in Kentucky, the superstition was that a pale red setting sun foretold illness," he said, squirming uneasily on the wooden seat. "Most of the time one can rule their life by such notions as that."

Faye turned troubled eyes toward Gayland. She did not need superstitious hogwash to cloud her thoughts. There was already enough to worry about. She ignored his statement and placed the rifle on the floor before turning to crawl into the back of the wagon, where she found Celia lying on a pallet of blankets, her copper-red hair spread around her pale face. With her delicate constitution Celia had not been able to carry a baby to term. Two miscarriages had been enough, and she and Gayland had ceased trying.

Not wanting to disturb Celia, Faye eased herself down to the floor beside her and picked up a book, but in the dim light she could not see it well enough to read. Nor could she concentrate with her traitorous thoughts drifting to Joe Harrison, to the wondrous feeling of his muscled arm about her waist and the desire that had swelled within.

Forcing her thoughts elsewhere, Faye looked about her, grimacing at the way she was being forced to travel. The wagon was a boxlike cart nearly as long as an ordinary bedroom and so wide that she could stretch herself out full length across the body. The top and sides were covered with osnaburg sheeting—a cloth made of flax or tow. It made excellent wagon covers. Rain could not soak through the cloth, and it was so cheap that one could well afford to use its double thickness, which served to keep out the wind as well as the rain. The front of the wagon had a small windowlike space at the end that was left open, but could be securely closed with curtains that buttoned at the side.

Underneath the cart hung buckets, the churn, lanterns, water kegs and farming tools. Pots and pans, towels, clothing, baskets and rifles were all kept inside. No beds were used on the trail. Pallets of blankets, which could be easily rolled up and stored during the day, sufficed.

The floors of the wagon curved up at the ends, making it almost impossible for the goods to fall out, even on the roughest roads. The wagon body could double as a boat when needed and could be counted on to float when crossing the rivers.

Hearing the shout of the wagon master, Faye was drawn to the entrance at the rear of the wagon. Easing aside the flap, she looked out and saw that the wagon master was leading the caravan into a circle, and they would soon be setting up camp for the night.

Waiting and watching, Faye observed how each wagon overlapped the other end and thus formed a continuous barricade. A few of the children were already walking about, gathering wood and buffalo chips for fuel. Faye got a glimpse of Joe Harrison as he stood amid a small group of men, cracking jokes. For a moment his eyes moved to her wagon, and when he saw her looking at him, Faye's insides grew strangely warm.

"Faye?"

At the sound of Celia's voice, Faye jerked away from the window. "We've arrived at camp for the night," she announced, then bent over the small form lying on the blankets. "*Comment vas-tu?* Gayland has already got a nice fire going. I think you'd feel much better if you got a breath of fresh air."

"Yes, I'm sure I would," Celia said, rising to a sitting position, her copper hair cascading over her shoulders. "I've disappointed Gayland enough on this trip. It seems you and my husband have had to do all the work."

In an effort to be strong for the two of them, Faye embraced Celia and hugged her fondly. "Gayland understands," she said softly. "He's special, you know. There aren't many men like him around."

In Faye's mind's eye, she tried to envision Joe being as gentle and as wonderful to her as Gayland was to Celia. But surely he did not know the meaning of gentleness. He only enjoyed teasing and tormenting! He was not a gentleman.

"Yes, I know," Celia said, easing from Faye's embrace. "And I must be the best wife that I can. Enough of this childish behavior. Tonight I will turn a new leaf. I shall not complain again about this terrible adventure."

"Nor shall I," Faye said, joining in the camaraderie, growing closer each day to Celia and Gayland. They felt as close as kin at a time when her only relative was a brother who had his church to occupy his mind and time. Would he be able to include her in his life? He had chosen to leave the family long ago to serve God.

Searching through the pots and pans, Celia handed one to Faye as she climbed from the wagon. A knot rose in her throat and her footsteps faltered as she looked up to find Joe Harrison's eyes set on her. A hot blush rose to her cheeks. Even when he wasn't tormenting her with words, he was humiliating her with his eyes.

Lifting her chin defiantly, Faye walked on toward the fire that Gayland was laying with kindling beside their wagon.

Chapter Two

Campfires blazed beside each of the covered wagons after the evening meal had been consumed. Beans had been placed with buffalo meat in big pots and were now in the hot ashes of the fires to cook overnight. Most all of the travelers were gathered around a large fire in the center of the campsite to socialize. Some sat on the ground as others stood close to the fire while songs were being sung to the accompaniment of a mouth organ. Plenty of scalding hot coffee from tin cups was being enjoyed.

With a fringed shawl draped around her shoulders, Faye sat beside Celia, sipping tea made from wild sassafras roots and watching Gayland, who stood with several men on the opposite side of the fire. They were discussing the coming day. A herd of grazing buffalo had been seen just before reaching this evening's campsite, and the men had decided to remain camped the next day to hunt and dry and cure the meat.

They had recently learned that the farther they traveled into Arkansas, the fewer buffalo would be found. Tallow-whackers, white hunters and outlaws who made a business of slaughtering buffalo, were rapidly destroying the dwindling herds.

The singing now over, Faye listened in on the soldiers' conversations. The rising number of outlaws was a growing cause for alarm. Many fugitives from justice and other desperate characters of the worst kind had come to the Ozarks where there was no law. Some made whiskey, and some specialized in horse theft. Others lived by hunting and trapping and selling pelts to the New Orleans market where they commanded a good price.

The United States Army had established itself at Fort Smith near the Three Forks of the Arkansas River to assist in reclaiming the country from the outlaws and to keep peace with the Indians. Alone in the wilderness, the pioneers quickly found that it was best to settle near the established fort.

Faye looked over to see Celia smother a yawn behind her hand, and gave her a pensive stare. "Celia, if you need to retire for the night, don't stay here by the fire on my account," she murmured. "I don't think I could go to sleep just yet." She cast her eyes downward. "I have a lot on my mind. Time does not help in relieving my burden of sadness...or the emptiness I feel over the loss of my parents. It's worse at times like this when families are together, singing and laughing beside the fire.''

Celia placed her tin cup on the ground and slipped an arm around Faye's shoulder. ''Time does eventually heal all wounds,'' she said reassuringly. She hugged Faye tightly to her bosom. ''You will see. In time, you will be able to accept it.''

Gayland lumbered over and knelt down beside Celia, running a hand sensually along her back and across the delicate curve of her buttocks in a silent message of desire. Turning from Faye, Celia swayed against her husband as he helped her to her feet.

Without looking up, Celia smoothed some stray strands of hair back from her brow. ''Honey, Gayland and I have some things to discuss in private,'' she whispered, blushing. ''Give us some time alone in our wagon? I'll open the flap once our conversation is concluded.'' She then bent down and cupped Faye's chin in the softness of her tiny hand. ''Will you be all right?''

Faye felt a blush rise to her cheeks. She well knew that her presence had come between Celia and her husband. She realized more and more that she no longer belonged to anyone or anything.

But she could not let Celia know how acutely lonely she felt. Celia was the sort who would feel to blame and would try to make things right, and nobody could make things right for Faye.

"*Oui*, I'll be fine," Faye murmured, forcing a smile. "Please go on. I do love sitting by the fire."

"I'm glad to hear you say that," Celia said, crinkling her ivory face into a sweet grin. "See? You are already beginning to adjust!"

Faye patted Celia's cheek fondly. "*Oui*, I am adjusting," she lied. "I will be all right."

Celia gave Faye a lingering smile, then took Gayland's hand as he helped her up. Faye watched with longing as Celia fell into step beside Gayland, their arms locked around each other, until they disappeared inside the wagon and closed the flap at the end. Never had Faye felt so alone as at that moment.

Squirming uneasily, Faye set her tin cup on the ground and rose to her feet. She had a need to take a walk to help shed her pent-up emotions.

With determination in her step, she went to the wagon and took a lighted lantern down from the wagon tongue. Drawing her shawl more snugly around her shoulders, she left the camp and walked into the outer fringes of the forest.

Starlight, pale and cold, silhouetted the ragged oaks of the ridge overhead. Water cascaded over a rocky falls somewhere close beside Faye where the Arkansas River ran crisp and cold in the dark. When she heard the rich bass of bullfrogs and the staccato chirping of crickets, memories of the Mississippi River clouded her thoughts. As she drew closer to the water, she walked beneath gnarled cedars that grew precariously from the sides of the sheer cliffs.

When she arrived at the riverbank, she held her lantern high and saw a dense fog clinging like a fallen cloud over the water. The buzzing of mosquitoes now drowned out the other night noises as they buzzed around her head.

Suddenly a loud shriek, as though someone were in pain, tore through the darkened forest around her. She recognized the distinct cry of a mountain lion, and goose bumps rose on her flesh as she turned with a start. She had heard the same cry one other time just as they had crossed the Arkansas border. At that time she had been warned that mountain lions were not the only predators that roamed the bottomlands of this territory, but also black bears.

Never more afraid in her life, her heart beat rapidly. Unable to tell just how close the mountain lion was, Faye clutched hard the handle of her lantern and shawl and turned and began to run through the forest. Frantic, she peered through the darkness in all directions, but nowhere did she see any signs of the campfire.

Cold, hard fear formed a solid lump in the pit of her stomach as she ran blindly beneath the low-hanging gnarled limbs of oaks, through brush, and over fallen logs. Her sides ached from the exertion, and she momentarily closed her eyes and took a deep, ragged breath, then was thrown off balance when she was suddenly caught up in a pair of very powerful arms.

With a crash, the lantern fell to the ground, the glass shattering into bits and pieces. The fire began to spread across the dried leaves that had fallen from the trees the previous autumn.

With a reflexive jerk, Faye loosed herself and stomped wildly at the flames that spread quickly from one leaf to another. The small fire smoldered, she caught sight of familiar moccasins and deerskin pants. Her insides recoiled when in the pale light of the moon seeping through the leaves overhead, she saw the amused smile and the hauntingly dark eyes of Joe Harrison as he stood there, looking down at her. His hair hung in sleek black strands to his shoulders, his silhouette wondrously muscled against the backdrop of night.

Where his buckskin shirt gaped open in front, Faye could see the crisp, dark fronds of his chest hair, and something undefinable stirred within her. Something made her want to twine her fingers through his hair and feel the muscles of his flesh against her skin.

"You!" she gasped, angrily collecting her thoughts. "*Monsieur*, always it's you!" She gestured toward her broken lantern and the burning leaves. "Do you see what you caused? You not only broke my lantern, but you may be the cause for the whole forest to catch fire!"

Joe lifted her by her shoulders and bodily stood her aside, then kicked at the ashes at his feet, making sure the fire was out. "You blame me for your careless behavior?" he said hotly. "Good Lord, Faye, what are you doing wandering so far from the campsite? Surely Gayland Johnston warned you of the dangers."

Spreading his long, lean legs and placing his hands on his hips, he glared down at her. "Or do you make it a habit of not listening?" he growled. "Have you always done exactly what you wanted? But, of course, more than once you have proved that you do."

Faye stood her ground and tried to calm her bothered heart by taking several deep breaths, then dared him with a stubborn tilt of her chin.

"It is none of your concern what I do, or why I do it," she said icily. "Why on earth do you persist in making me your business? You were paid to escort the wagon train, not me personally."

"Ma'am," Joe said just as coldly. "I'm afraid hell would have to freeze over before I'd escort you anywhere. It is my duty to see to your welfare the same as the others. If you think that I have singled you out personally, you are very badly mistaken."

Hurt by his lecture, Faye was at a loss for words. Then feeling humiliated, she turned and stomped away.

But another scream of the mountain lion, this time sounding closer than before, made her gasp loudly with fright. Her footsteps faltered.

When a strong arm slipped suddenly about her waist, she tensed and tried to shove it away. But she succeeded only in causing him to tighten his grip, imprisoning her beside him as he began walking her toward the camp.

"I truly see no reason why we have chosen to behave as enemies," Joe said stiffly. "It seems we got off on the wrong foot with one another. Let's at least behave civilly. It's a long journey to Fort Smith. Behaving this way toward one another is quite awkward, to say the least, while with the others of this wagon train. Some might even interpret our behavior as that done purposely to hide feelings of romance. Now do you honestly want people to take notions such as those about us?"

Faye's eyes widened as she listened intently to his every word and tried to find meaning behind each of them. Feelings of romance, indeed! She gave him a haughty glance and kept walking as quickly as she could.

Relieved to see the campfire ahead, Faye managed to squirm from Joe's grip. She half ran to the campsite, but her hopes for escape dwindled when she saw that the flap was still closed on the wagon.

Stiffening when Joe came to her side, she did not look his way when he spoke into her ear.

"Now be careful," he whispered. "Someone might see us together and get the wrong idea."

His hot breath stirred unwanted pleasure within her, Faye fought a blush that was trying to surface. A sigh of relief escaped her when Bart Dobbs sauntered over and locked an arm playfully around Joe's shoulder, giving Faye a slow glance.

"Sweet on 'er, eh, Joe?" Bart teased right in front of her. "Can't say as I blame you. Pretty young thing and mighty available, ain't she?"

Feeling the hair raise at the nape of her neck, Faye shot Joe, then Bart, an angry look, then fled back into the outer fringes of the forest. At the sound of footsteps behind her, she did not turn to see who followed her. She knew that it would be Joe.

If only the circumstances were different, she would turn to him and offer herself to him. She longed to be drawn into his arms. She needed comforting and reassurances that life would be sweet again.

But not from one so crude, not from the hired hand. Again his fingers were brutal on her shoulders as he grabbed her and flung her around to face him.

"Now, dammit, Faye," he stormed. "I've led you from the forest once tonight, I don't want to have to do it again."

Tears pooled in her eyes as she looked up at him. "Just leave me alone," she said, unable to stop a sob that broke from deep within her throat. "This is all so unbearable to me, and you aren't making it any easier." She doubled her hands into fists at her sides. "Let me be! You aren't the sort to understand anything."

Joe dropped his hand and raked his fingers nervously through his hair. "Just what sort do you think I am?" he said thickly. "God, woman, you look at me as though I am a savage without any brains. Is that so?"

Hearing the wounded tone of his voice, Faye felt suddenly ashamed. She knew down deep inside that he was only trying to help her each time he had come to her assistance, yet she had not wanted to appear as though she needed him. She wanted to learn to take care of herself. Her pride demanded it.

Turning her back to him, Faye swallowed another sob and wiped the tears from her eyes. "I apologize for how I have behaved toward you," she murmured. Then her stomach became strangely queasy as he placed his hands to her waist and slowly turned her to face him again.

"Can we call a truce?" he asked softly. "Can we at least be friends?"

"*Oui*, that would be nice," Faye said, nodding.

"Then let's go back and sit beside the fire," Joe said, guiding her from the forest. He looked toward Gayland and Celia's wagon and saw the flap was still closed and wished for the first time that he had his own wagon.

Now that Faye Poincaré was in his blood, there was no getting her out of it. Surely she was nothing like Kathryn. Surely she could be trusted. No matter their differences, somehow they would eventually experience the wonders of kisses and embraces.

"I'll get you a cup of coffee," Joe blurted, feeling clumsy now that he had Faye's dutiful attention. "You just sit right down here close to the fire. You look as though you may have caught a chill."

Faye's hands went to her shoulders, just now realizing that she had lost her shawl. "Coffee would be fine," she said searching Joe's face as he momentarily stared down at her.

Quickly, she turned away from him and sat down on the ground close to the fire. She welcomed the warmth of the hot coals near her cold skin. She welcomed even more the cup of coffee that Joe offered her as he sat down beside her.

"*Merci*," Faye murmured, her voice strained as she struggled to hide the tumultuous feelings that his very presence aroused inside her.

Joe sipped his own cup of coffee, staring into the flames of the fire, wanting to break the strained silence between him and Faye. She was unnerving him as only one other woman in his life had done.

His thoughts went to Kathryn. She had come to Fort Smith with her father, the commanding officer. It hadn't taken long for Joe to single her out as quite different from the women who worked the saloons outside the walls of the fort. She had been educated and refined. She had been beautiful and desirable. That she had fallen in love with him had been almost too much for Joe to believe.

But it hadn't taken long for him to realize that Kathryn could not accept the life of the wilderness. Finally she had returned to the city, leaving Joe alone on their wedding day. When Kathryn's father had come to Joe and had told him the facts, Joe had sworn never to love again.

"So, Faye, what brings you to Arkansas?" he blurted, sloshing the coffee around inside his tin cup.

Faye took another slow sip, finding it hard to speak of her parents' deaths. "I'm going to go live with my brother," she murmured. "My parents—they died not long ago. Michael is all the kin that I have left. Celia and Gayland Johnston were kind enough to become my paid companions and included me on their journey to the Ozarks, so here I am."

"You're from New Orleans?" Joe asked stiffly, suspecting all along that she was a city girl by her manner.

"*Oui*, New Orleans," Faye said, setting the empty tin cup on the ground beside her. She turned her eyes to him. "*Et vous?* What brought you to the Ozarks?"

"My father. He's a retired lieutenant in the army." Joe said, placing his empty cup aside. He drew his legs up before him and hugged them with his arms. "Since I was a young lad, I've been forced to learn the life of a wanderer. My father moved from fort to fort, never staying in one place for very long. I became a wanderer in the true sense of the word at age eighteen when I broke away from my family, but when Fort Smith was first established and my father was stationed there for a short time before his retirement, I followed, you might say for the adventure. I had always wanted to see what all the fuss was about when people talked about the Ozarks. My father and mother lived just beyond the fort walls before they moved back to Boston."

"You didn't say who all lived with you in your parents' house," Faye said softly, trying to draw answers from him. "Was there just you and your parents?" Or was there a woman? she wanted to know.

"No, I didn't say," Joe said stiffly, evading her obvious intent. Though he was damned attracted to her, he'd vowed to be careful with all women.

Embarrassed by his bluntness, Faye cast a longing look toward the closed wagon flap. It appeared as though she must suffer with Joe Harrison for a while longer.

Her brows drew together in a frown. Did it have to take Gayland and Celia so long just to make love? Was it truly so wonderful that one did not wish to leave the other's arms?

Joe followed Faye's gaze and wondered at her thoughts. Had Faye ever made love before? Probably not. Undoubtedly she was used to suave, fancy gentlemen callers. Joe had never worn fancy suits and ruffled shirts.

Long ago Joe had found the lure of the wilderness much more to his liking than city living. Several years ago he had become acquainted with Bart Dobbs, who had taught him the art of hunting and trading, tracking and scouting. He had known then that he had found his place in life. The only thing that had been lacking was the right woman.

Faye jerked her head around. Combing her fingers through her dark hair, she glanced nervously over at Joe. "Tell me about the Ozarks," she encouraged softly. "Why do you like this region so much?"

"This land is seductive like no woman," Joe began almost dreamily. "There's wild game aplenty, and the landscape can clean take a man's breath away." He gestured with a swing of his right hand. "Here you will see steep hillsides, there a twisting valley, over yonder grassy plateaus. Some call the Ozarks hills, others call them mountains, but as you have seen, the mountains aren't so high as the valleys are deep."

He frowned deeply. "I do everything within my power to protect the land and the settlers," he said softly. "Though I refused to join the army, I do my part as a scout and tracker. I want to see that everyone is protected from outlaws."

His eyes grew dark. "Yes, I try to do my part," he said thickly. "Though there are those who try to get in my way. Those who preach that the vigilantes have the God-given right to hang outlaws get my blood boiling! An orderly government is needed to enforce the law and to keep peace!"

Laughing awkwardly, he glanced over at Faye. "Now, I didn't mean to bore you," he apologized, his expression softening.

Faye's eyes were wide with wonder. "You're not boring me," she said quietly. "Tell me more about the vigilantes. What is their purpose?"

"Their purpose?" Joe said with a snarl. "To cause aggravation in the community. They think they are the ones born to rule. They are members of a self-appointed citizen group who called themselves a vigilance committee. This committee takes the law into its own hands. Hanging is their brand of quick punishment."

He picked up a twig and threw it into the fire, frustrated by the mere thought of the vigilantes. "But enough about them," he said dryly. "Tell me some more about yourself. What do you think of this fair land?"

Faye held her head back, letting her hair tumble in a dark sheen across her shoulders and down to her waist. She viewed the stars, knowing that they were the same in her native city. "Oh, how I miss New Orleans," she said, sighing forlornly. "I imagine that even right this moment a ball is being attended by my friends. Oh, it would be pure heaven to be dressed in silk again and have the scent of magnolias on my skin."

A cold wind found its way to Joe's heart. He gave Faye an angry glare, then moved quickly to his feet. "Tomorrow will come bright and early," he said blandly. "The buffalo hunt will be arduous. I must get my rest."

He looked over at Celia and Gayland's wagon and saw that the flap was finally raised. His gaze was sharp as he looked down at Faye and offered her a hand, then helped her up from the ground. "I shall take you to your wagon and bid you good-night," he said dryly.

Faye was stunned by his sudden coldness. Haughtily, she pulled away from him. "Your escort is not needed," she snapped. "*Bon soir, monsieur.*"

Storming away from Joe, Faye was near to tears. Her first impression of him had been correct, she told herself. He was not the sort she should associate with.

Yet she could not help it. She knew that even tonight when she drifted off to sleep, he would be there in her dreams.

Climbing into the wagon, Faye tiptoed to her bedroll at the far end of the wagon from where Celia and

Gayland were peacefully snuggling together. Slipping her dress over her head and placing it close beside her, she crawled between her blankets, wishing she could stop the furious beating of her heart.

Squeezing her eyes together tightly, she tried to lose the picture of Joe in her mind's eye.

Joe sauntered over to the dying campfire near which Bart Dobbs and the soldiers were already snoozing in bedrolls tossed haphazardly over the ground. Grumbling, he pulled off his moccasins and removed his gun belt.

"She's so thick in your blood there's no gettin' free of her, ain't she?" Bart taunted, jabbing Joe in the ribs with his fist. "You never learn, do you? Why cain't you do like me? I just love 'em and leave 'em. There's plenty waiting for us back home. The saloon ladies are aplenty nowadays. Wowie, some are lookers, and they don't ask nothin' of you except for one night's lovin' and what you're willin' to pay for it."

Joe spread his blankets on the ground and pulled a buffalo hide up to his chin. "Dammit, get back to sleep, will you?" he growled, unable to stop his gaze from traveling to Faye's wagon.

Damn her! Damn the city woman who already missed the social niceties. In time, she would want to return, just the same as Kathryn had....

Chapter Three

The noonday sun filtered through the high canopies of leaves overhead. The silver-lined leaves of the cottonwoods rustled noisily in the breeze, sounding like rain, and the cottony seeds drifted down to settle in the earth's nooks and crannies.

Faye was kneeling beside the river, washing clothes. Wringing out a pillowcase, she noticed a stirring in the ground close beside her. Scarcely breathing, she laid the pillowcase in a wicker basket behind her and watched the dirt being formed into a crude tunnel by an invisible hand.

Faye knew that it was a mole and continued to watch. She waited quietly as the small rodent with its gray coat emerged from the earth, oblivious of an audience. Its cheeks were puffed out as if it were a squirrel packing nuts. It blew the fine dark earth out of its mouth and repeated this action again and again until there was a ring of black, powdery soil on the ground.

Then it ducked back into the hole and burrowed its underground cavern in another direction away from Faye.

Faye smiled in amusement and lifted her head to take in the scenery on the other side of the river. The trees bent over the bank like lovers reaching out to one another, and wildflowers created a carpet of gold and scarlet, pink and purple along the riverbank. An elusive ivory-billed woodpecker was perched on the side of a tree, its knocking insistent and noisy. From the branch of an ash tree a solitary bird sent out high, thin, single notes, and humming insects swarmed around cattails at the water's edge.

Everything was beautiful, but Faye could not truly enjoy it. Gayland had grown ill in the middle of the night, his body racked with hard chills and high fever, and had been taken to old Doc Rose's wagon to be isolated from the rest of the travelers. Doc Rose had been welcomed on the wagon train just outside New Orleans. A widower and a man of great medicinal talents, he had offered his services and his wagon to anyone who fell ill on the journey.

"Gayland has bilious fever," Doc Rose had said, his shaggy gray eyebrows knitted together into a deep frown. "He's in for a rocky road ahead. With his constant vomiting and diarrhea, it's next to impossible to administer internal relief. He'll just have to ride it out."

Celia had accompanied Gayland to Doc Rose's wagon and would remain with her husband to look to his comfort until his health improved enough to return to his own wagon, even though there was a threat that she would also contract the fierce malady.

Faye had been given total charge of their wagon. It was now up to her to see that Gayland and Celia's belongings made it to Fort Smith.

Dipping the last of the bedding soiled by Gayland into the water, Faye rinsed lye soap from it, then took it from the water and wrung it out. In the not so far distance she could hear the shouts of the men and the gun blasts of the buffalo slaughter. Early that morning, a herd of buffalo had been spied grazing as close as the next rise in the land. No one had even stopped to eat breakfast. The hunt had begun as soon as the last suspender was slipped over a shoulder.

Smoothing a lock of hair back from her perspiration-streaked brow, she placed the wet bedding into her wicker basket. At the sound of another gun blast, Faye stiffened. It was not in her nature to want anything killed, not even the buffalo so vital to their survival. Still, something drew her to the hunt...

Abruptly, she stood straight. Joe Harrison! Surely he would be the best of all the hunters. With her nails digging into the palms of her hands, Faye tried to deny the truth.

Leaning over the crystal clear water, she looked at her reflection. In the confusion of the early morning, she had not bothered much with her appearance. Her hair had been quickly brushed and drawn back with a ribbon. She had slipped into a skirt and blouse, and had rolled the sleeves up past her elbows.

Pinching her cheeks to add some color to them and rolling the sleeves of her blouse down, Faye gave herself one last glance in the water's mirror. She certainly did not look at all like the girl who had resembled a princess in her ball gowns, but she did look presentable enough.

Grabbing her basket, she hurried back to her wagon. Once she had strung a clothesline from their wagon to the one next to them, she hung the wet clothes in the hot sun. Not a cloud dotted the sky on this perfect summer day. The clothes would be dry by evening.

At the thought of the sun's setting, a cold fear formed in the pit of her stomach. She would be alone in this wilderness. Throughout the entire night, perhaps for many nights. Her insides began to churn. Nervously, she pulled the ribbon from her hair and shook the long strands to hang loosely down her back.

The other women in the camp busied themselves with all the chores that could be done while the wagons were halted. Looking from side to side, Faye saw no one free to accompany her, so she grabbed a rifle and began walking toward the rise of land where she would find the men hard at work after the kill. She would watch for only a moment, then return to her own chores at hand.

A red-tailed hawk patrolled the sky overhead as Faye's legs began to ache. The distance was much farther than it appeared. As she reached the rise, she could see a long range of rugged, timbered mountains on the horizon. And behind the bluff to the east, wide meadows covered with lush grass and sprinkled with white and yellow wildflowers spread all the way to the foothills of another magnificent range rising to the clear blue sky.

Faye sighed in awe of the pristine beauty of the Ozarks. If the free land itself were not an attraction to settlers, surely the beauty could be.

Suddenly the beauty of the scene was spoiled by the lifeless bodies of the slaughtered buffalo that lay across the land, their blood like crimson velvet as the men skillfully removed the skins.

Faye's footsteps faltered at the gruesome sight. She turned her eyes away, glad that there would be no more shooting. As though inviting their execution, a few stray buffalo still stood not far from the activity.

And then Faye heard a loud snort from somewhere close by. Her spine stiffening, she turned slowly around, and everything within her grew cold as she found herself staring point-blank into the eyes of a buffalo bull. He stood at the edge of a dip in the land not far from where she stood.

She took a shaky step backward and looked beyond the animal, searching frantically for anyone who might see her to safety, but most were too absorbed in the work to notice.

Except for one man.

Joe had paused long enough to wipe beads of perspiration from his brow, letting his eyes scan the land, watching the buffalo, never trusting them. His insides grew numb when he saw Faye edging back from a buffalo bull, fear frozen in her eyes. "Dammit," he uttered, angrily jabbing his bloody *dague*, point side down, into the ground. He gave Bart a nervous glance. "Bart, take a look over yonder. Seems we've one more buffalo to kill."

Bart looked over his shoulder, then was taken aback when he saw the buffalo challenging Faye. "That stupid woman," he gasped. "What in hell is she doin' here? Doesn't she know her place?"

"Seems not," Joe said, quickly picking up his rifle. "Come on, Bart. We'd better move quickly. Who's to say when that bull will charge? His eyes are set on her, that's for sure."

Bart chuckled beneath his breath as he grabbed his rifle. "She's attractin' all sorts of attentions these days," he mocked. "I know another fella whose eyes bug right outta his head every time he looks at her. Now I just wonder what his name might be?''

Joe cast Bart an angry stare as they moved quickly. ''This isn't the time for that, Bart,'' he said flatly. ''The lady's in a peck of trouble.''

Joe and Bart moved briskly across the land. When Faye's eyes met Joe's she grimaced, for it seemed that again she was at his mercy. He would truly tease and torment her.

But this was no time to worry about bantering with a man. An animal was her main cause for danger at this moment, and the way the buffalo was digging a hoof in the ground, snorting and wheezing, she knew to expect him to charge at any moment. Something told her not to take another step.

Pale and trembling, Faye focused her eyes on Joe and Bart, hoping that their expertise with this sort of situation would be enough to save her life. She watched as they moved closer and closer.

''There's a western breeze, Bart,'' Joe said, loud enough for only Bart to hear. ''Let's make a slow turn eastward. As long as he doesn't know we're here and Faye stands quiet, I think we'll get him with no trouble.''

''Yeah, if she stands quiet,'' Bart scoffed, moving slowly eastward with Joe. ''Any moment I expect her to turn and run for her life.''

''I think she's too scared to do anything,'' Joe said, laughing to himself. ''But dammit, I've got to say, she's even prettier when her eyes are wide with fright.''

Bart groaned. "You've got it bad," he growled. "I'd have thought Kathryn would've been enough for you. Now you're fallin' for another one just like 'er.''

Joe frowned. "Yeah, another one just like Kathryn," he grumbled. "I'll have to keep reminding myself of that.''

Tense, Joe loaded and primed his rifle. "Ready, Bart?" he said, his jaw firmly set.

"Ready," Bart said, dropping to the ground along with Joe.

They crept on all fours toward the animal. When within close proximity, Joe and Bart lay prostrate on the ground, pushed their rifles before them and scooted still closer until they came near enough to fire.

Together they leveled their slim, heavy weapons and aimed. "Now, Faye!" Joe shouted. "Take off and run as fast as those pretty legs will carry you!"

Faye received the message loud and clear, ignoring his reference to her legs, which he had not, nor ever would, see. Her knees weak, her heartbeat erratic, she whipped her skirt around and began running.

Joe took half a breath and checked his aim, then without pause pulled the trigger. The rifle roared and recoiled against his shoulder. The first shot pierced the thickness of the buffalo's chest cavity, but, dammit, he had missed its heart!

Bart aimed and fired, entirely missing the buffalo, something quite unusual for the skilled hunter.

"Dammit!" Joe gasped, jumping to his feet, watching in horror as the buffalo snorted and began running in Faye's direction. Then, as though crazed, the animal made a sudden turn and began running toward him and Bart.

Standing with his legs widespread and his rifle loaded and ready to fire again, Joe held his piece stiffly with one hand, aimed and fired.

But the animal turned repeatedly, not fazed by even the second wound.

Joe looked at Faye. She had stopped and turned, thinking the buffalo was dead, when, in truth, she had discovered that the wounded buffalo had circled and was headed in her direction again.

Faye felt a light-headedness sweep through her. She could not fight it. As her knees buckled beneath her, she crumpled to the ground, lost in a void of blackness as she fainted.

"Good Lord!" Joe said, his voice sounding strangled. He took one more steady aim, his heartbeat wild, and this time when he shot, he hit the animal's heart.

His fingers trembling, his brow a mass of perspiration, he watched the animal pitch, with a sudden tremendous bellow, headlong to the ground. The animal made a few convulsive struggles, then expired.

Joe ran to Faye and grabbed her in his arms. Holding her close to his heaving chest, he ran with her back to her wagon. After placing her on a pallet of blankets, he reached for a basin of water and a washcloth and began smoothing the damp cloth across her pale brow. When her eyes fluttered open, he smiled nervously down at her and placed a hand gently to her cheek.

"Woman, what am I going to do with you?" he whispered.

Faye's eyes opened wildly. She looked blankly up into Joe's face, then looked around her. "What happened?" she gasped, again looking up at Joe. "How did I get here?"

Then a cold sweat popped out on Faye's brow as she realized just how close the buffalo had been to her before she had . . .

"Oh, non," she moaned. "I fainted. Never before in my life have I fainted."

A pink blush rose to her cheeks. Embarrassed anew, she lowered her eyes, knowing that once again Joe Harrison had come to her rescue. The reasons to thank him were increasing one by one, like the notches in a gunman's belt denoting each victory. But the victories were Joe's, not hers.

"Well, I would guess that most women would faint if they were about to be trampled by a buffalo bull,"

Joe said, trying to reassure her. But the fire in her eyes made him realize that he most surely had assumed wrong.

Pushing herself up into a sitting position, Faye narrowed her eyes, again seeing him as someone she could so easily loathe. Not only did he see her as a woman with no sense, but that was how he most surely saw all women.

"You would be the sort who would expect a woman to faint in the face of danger," she said, folding her arms across her chest. "And because I did this one time, you will expect me to repeat the performance for you another time, won't you? *Monsieur*, I can assure you I won't entertain you in such a way again!"

Joe raked his fingers nervously through his long black hair, finding it harder and harder to understand her. He would have expected to have received a sweet, gentle thank-you from her beautiful lips, but instead he had unleashed an untamed fury.

Taking a step backward, he decided that it was better if she behaved haughtily toward him. It was much safer that way.

"Well, I certainly don't need a repeat performance," he said softly. "As I see it, these past few days you've gotten in enough trouble to last you a lifetime."

Faye blinked her eyes nervously, knowing that what he said was true. Never in her life had she felt so foolish and clumsy.

Smoothing her skirt, she let her gaze follow the movement of her hands, gasping as she saw how they shook. In her mind's eye, she was seeing the buffalo charging her. She was seeing the blood spread across the land where the other buffalo had been slaughtered. She shuddered violently.

Placing his hands on her shoulders and squeezing his fingers into her flesh, he glowered down at her. "Why in hell were you there in the first place?" he said between clenched teeth.

Faye was taken aback by the venom in his tone. She glared at him. "Why was I where?" she asked, her voice trailing off as she saw concern in his dark, fathomless eyes.

A sensual heat warmed her flesh. His fingers no longer pained her, but instead tormented her in another way, in the way a man stirred feelings within a woman by his mere touch and presence.

"You know what I'm talking about," Joe said, his voice strained as he took in her softening gaze. She could not hide the fact that she was as troubled by him as he was by her. "You shouldn't have been anywhere near those buffalo. The rest of the women were tending to womanly duties. Why weren't you?"

At his mention of other women and their duties, Faye smacked his hands away from her shoulders and rose to her feet. With an arm stiff with fury, she pointed toward the flap at the end of the wagon.

"You've got your own sorts of duties to perform, don't you?" she mimicked. "Leave me to mine. I'm certain no man would want to lower himself to even see what a woman does from morning to night."

"Ma'am, I didn't expect a thank-you from you, anyhow," he growled, edging his way around her. "Just keep your thank-yous to yourself. That suits me fine."

Bart Dobbs suddenly raised the flap at the end of the wagon and stuck his head inside. He held Faye's rifle in one hand, and a *dague* in the other. "Joe, you forgot your *dague*. Ma'am, your rifle."

He placed the weapons inside the wagon, then glanced nervously over his shoulder. "Joe, you best come on out here," he said, turning questioning eyes to Faye, then back to Joe. "Dark storm clouds are fast accumulating over the mountains. If we're going to finish up, we'd best get to it. It sure does look to me like a gulley-washer's coming this way."

"I'm coming gladly," Joe said, moving past Faye, then bending to grab his *dague*. He gave Faye a quiet, lingering look before he climbed from the wagon and walked briskly away with Bart.

"That's the damndest woman I've ever met," Joe said, his shoulders hunched in anger. "Though she is a city woman, something sets her apart from those sort. I guess it's her spirit. But dammit, I don't trust her.''

Bart chuckled as he glanced over at Joe. ''There's more to it than trust,'' he said, his green eyes twinkling. ''Joe, you want her so bad you can taste her. When you going to quit that infernal fussin' with her? It's gettin' you nowhere fast. Take the leap. You'll never know what she's really like if you don't.''

Joe rubbed his furrowed brow. ''Dammit, Bart, don't go preaching at me.''

Shaken, Faye stared at the void inside the wagon for a moment, then went and raised the flap at the end and peered up into the sky. Alarm spread inside her like wildfire. In the west, rain clouds were building up like purple satin pillows. She had been told that when rains came in the Ozarks, they could last for days. The rivers could even become impassable.

Angrily, she slapped the flap down and turned away just as a slight rumble of thunder was heard in the distant hills. It seemed to reach clean into her soul. Tonight she would be so alone, and a storm would make loneliness and fears so much worse.

Gayland's superstitious warnings came suddenly to mind. A pale red setting sun foretold illness. The

superstition had proved true. Gayland was ill. She ·
had almost been killed.

And now a menacing storm threatened her very
existence.

Chapter Four

Darkness had fallen over the land, and the storm that had lingered over the mountains for most of the afternoon and evening was just now rolling across the valley toward the circle of wagons. Incessant, jagged streaks of lightning lit up the sky, and claps of thunder echoed through the forest.

Faye paced the narrow space inside her wagon, wishing the storm was already over. The lightning was what she hated most. When she had been a small child she had seen lightning strike a house close to hers and burn it to the ground. Everyone within had been consumed in the flames. The memory brought back the horror.

She shook her head fitfully, knowing she should think of something else if she hoped to conquer the fear. Still, she jumped when a flash of lightning lit up the canvas on all sides of her.

Pulling the skirt of her cotton dress close around her, she determinedly turned up the wick in her kerosene lamp. As the flames spread on the soaked wick, a much brighter light flooded the wagon. Maybe now she would not notice the lightning as much.

She began pacing again, then stopped in midstep and looked nervously around her, feeling her acute aloneness and vulnerability. She would be easy prey for any of the woman-starved soldiers who were escorting the wagon train to Fort Smith. Once word had spread that Gayland was still ailing and that Celia still sat vigil at his side, it would become common knowledge that Faye was traveling alone.

Her gaze sought out her rifle. Her lips set in a willful line, she grabbed it and placed it where she would have easy access to it, then returned to her pacing, her petticoats swishing around her delicately tapered ankles.

After a sponge bath with perfumed soap, her hair freshly washed, and now in a clean cotton dress with a low bodice and lace trimming, she felt like a new person and tried not to think about the afternoon ordeal and Joe Harrison.

"Joe Harrison," Faye whispered, troubled by the way his name slipped so easily from her lips.

Joe had pitched his small tent close beside the communal fire. He sat alone inside his tent sipping coffee. A Jew's harp twanged from somewhere close by, and the air was still pleasantly heavy with the smell of cooked buffalo meat.

Fearing the storm, haste had been made to prepare the meat into pemmican, a process of drying the meat and pounding it fine, then mixing it with melted fat.

His stomach was comfortably full after eating buffalo tongue, a delicacy when baked over the fire and served with berries that had been gathered in the woods.

But even in his comfort, Joe was worrying about Faye. She had not joined the others for the evening meal. In fact, he had not seen her leave the wagon since he had left her.

Yet why should he worry about her? She must have her own supply of food. Most everyone on the trail carried within their wagons dried fruits, jerked beef, and homemade yeast cakes that had been baked in tin reflectors before the journey's start. There was always plenty of fresh butter from the churns jostled by the sway of the wagons.

He splashed the remainder of his coffee out the front of his tent and stretched out on his back on a thick layer of blankets.

His gaze went to the sky. He was dreading the storm. Bart had been right to say that it looked as if it would be a gulley-washer. Storms that lingered over the mountains always seemed to be the worst.

The creeks would rise, and the rivers would more than likely become impassable.

What then? The wagon train could be held up for days. The possibility of a delay in reaching Fort Smith gnawed at his gut. This was one time he wanted to get his duties of escorting a wagon train behind him. Once away from Faye Poincaré, perhaps he could forget her.

Moving his eyes slowly back to Faye's wagon, a keen pleasure swept through him when he saw her outline through the brightly lighted canvas. As she paced, his eyes followed her form, his loins burning with desire for her.

Dammit, didn't she know that she was visible to every man in the campsite? He could see the long tumble of her hair, the outline of her generous breasts, the tininess of her waist and the perfect line of her back.

The more Joe watched her, the faster his heart beat and the dryer his mouth became. He had never desired a woman as much as now.

Kneading his brow, he turned his eyes away, but like a magnet her restless silhouette was pulling his gaze back around. Again he watched and hungered for her. When he saw her lurch with fright at a great clap of thunder, he realized just what she must be going through. She was scared and she was alone.

A low wolf whistle from somewhere close by made Joe's insides grow numbly cold. He wasn't the only one watching Faye's restlessness. Surely she had an audience of many.

His jaw set, Joe grabbed his moccasins and thrust his feet into them. Without wasting time to pull on his shirt, he left his tent and hurried toward Faye's wagon, not caring if the men who were enjoying Faye's innocence saw him go to her. He had to tell her to douse the light or be fuel for some hungry man's fire before the night was over. If he couldn't have her, dammit, no one else would.

Everything within Faye had grown cold when she had heard an unknown man's unseemly whistle. Her fingers trembled as she reached for the rifle. Sitting down at the front end of the wagon, she aimed the loaded rifle point-blank at the closed flap. If any man got the notion that she would be dessert after his feast of buffalo tongue, he would soon see just how wrong he was!

Steadying her arm, she watched and waited.

Only footsteps away from Faye's wagon, Joe looked up into the sky as the first raindrops began to fall. Then suddenly the rain began to fall in torrents.

Blinded by nature's driving forces, Joe stumbled when he reached Faye's wagon. Clumsily he lurched headfirst through the opening. Catching his breath, he lifted his eyes, stunned speechless to find himself looking down the barrel of a rifle.

Faye jumped with a start at Joe's sudden entry into her wagon. She rose quickly to her feet as he still lay but halfway inside her wagon. Over the din of the downpour, she could hear the wind whipping the canvas, could feel the floor shimmy beneath her feet.

"What are you doing here?" she gasped. She knew that he must be getting soaked from the waist down, but wasn't sure if she should welcome his presence.

Suddenly a slow smile curved her lips. She was not the one who was clumsy this time. At this moment, no one could look as clumsy as Joe Harrison. Perhaps after this he would not be quite so arrogant.

Joe looked nervously into the barrel of the rifle, then up at Faye. He could tell that she was enjoying this and now wished that he had not bothered with coming to warn her about the show she was giving the soldiers. She had been right when she had earlier told him that she was not his concern. After this, she wouldn't be.

"Will you please lower that rifle, or are you planning to use it on me?" he said hoarsely.

Faye looked awkwardly at the rifle, realizing she had not lowered it even so much as an inch.

Laughing lightly, she considered him a moment. But a sudden, intense clap of thunder startled her so, her body jerked, causing her finger to involuntarily squeeze the trigger.

The kick of the heavy firearm knocked Faye to the floor of the wagon. Momentarily stunned, she sat there blinking. As the smoke cleared away, she was afraid to look. If she had killed him . . .

Joe had ducked when he had seen her finger grab for the trigger. Now everything was suddenly quiet except for Joe's harsh breathing intermixed with Faye's. He slowly raised his eyes, realizing that the ball from the rifle had missed him. He looked sideways and saw the hole in the canvas to his left where rain was now blowing in.

At once angry and relieved, he pulled himself on inside the wagon and stood dripping wet, his long, lean legs parted. His shoulders and head bent against the low ceiling, he glared down at Faye as she sat trembling at his feet, still clutching the rifle.

"You could have killed me," Joe growled, stooping and grabbing the rifle from her. "You stupid woman. Don't you know anything? What are you doing with a firearm if you don't even know how to handle one?"

He tossed the rifle aside and placed his hands on his hips, his bare chest heaving, the coal black hairs on his chest wet and kinky. Beneath the dancing light of the lamp, his skin had a wet golden sheen. Seeing him half-dressed made Faye's heart beat rapidly.

"That was sure a good way to welcome a man who was coming to see to your welfare," Joe continued hotly.

He nodded toward the kerosene lamp. The glass chimney was now blackened from the flames burning too high within. "If you don't turn that lamp down, you'll have two things to fight off," he stormed. "First, there's the men ogling you as they watch your silhouette in the bright lamplight through the canvas. Second, you're taking a chance of burning Gayland's wagon down with you in it if you don't screw the damned wick down."

Not used to being scolded by anyone, Faye grew pale under Joe's tongue-lashing. She was so taken aback by his anger and so mesmerized by his savage sort of handsomeness that she could not even find the strength to pull herself back up to her feet.

Stunned, she realized she had almost killed Joe Harrison and he had come to warn her of the danger. He had the right to scold her this time. He had the right to call her stupid and anything else that might fit the moment. This time she would not argue back.

She stared up at him, speechless, then her gaze moved slowly downward, taking in his soaked breeches that clung to him like a glove, revealing his God-given manliness at the juncture of his thighs.

Embarrassed, she forced her eyes lower, not wanting to let him know how the sight had stirred her insides into flaming passion.

"*Monsieur*, you're going to catch your death of pneumonia," she blurted, staring at his moccasins as he stood in a growing puddle.

"What?" Joe said, his voice filled with surprised outrage. "Here I am, lucky to be alive, and you're worrying about me taking pneumonia?"

He racked his fingers through his hair and turned to leave, but he halted when a soft, weak voice spoke again from behind him.

"*S'il vous plaît*, don't go," Faye said, hugging herself as a fresh clap of thunder rocked the wagon. She closed her eyes to the blazing lightning. The wind whined and whistled menacingly as it blew around the outside corners of the wagon.

Joe doubled his fists, knowing that he should leave. But something made him turn slowly around to look down at her.

His heart skipped a beat when he saw her cover her eyes and attempt in vain to control her body's trembling. Damn, if she wasn't scared to death of the storm! At this moment, she looked like a small child, alone in the world and so very, very vulnerable.

She *was* alone, and she *was* vulnerable. But she was much more than a mere *child*.

Without a moment's hesitation, Joe went to the lamp and lowered its wick, then he moved to his knees before Faye.

Gently, he took her hands and eased them from her face. He placed a forefinger to her chin and lifted it so their eyes could meet and hold.

His mouth went dry when he saw the fear in Faye's eyes give way to longing. Her lips were too close. She smelled too sweet.

"You cared so much?" she murmured, swallowing hard, fighting the yearning that was building within her. "You came because you cared?"

Faye's words shook Joe back to reality. He did care. He had come to protect her from the other men, but maybe it was he who posed the true threat.

Dropping his hand, Joe backed away from her. "It just didn't seem right that someone didn't come and warn you about the dangers," he said. "Alone here, you are at the mercy of who knows what?"

He eyed the rifle warily. "But I'll be the first one to tell Gayland to teach you the art of handling a firearm once he's back on his feet," he said, then his eyes gleamed as a slow smile lifted his lips. "At least you'll have some ventilation to give you relief from the afternoon heat now that you've got another hole in the canvas."

Relieved that he wasn't poking fun at her clumsiness, Faye rose to her feet. She shook the wrinkles out of her skirt, then looked at Joe's wet breeches.

"You *will* catch your death of cold in those things," she said, her face growing hot with a blush when she realized that it sounded as though she was asking him to remove them. "But of course you're not going to stay all that long, anyway. You'll soon be in your tent, changing into something dry."

Joe rose slowly, standing so close to her that he could again smell the sweetness of her hair and her skin. "Do you want me to leave?" he asked huskily. "Or would you rather I stay until the storm passes?"

A great crash of thunder from somewhere close by made goose bumps crawl along Faye's flesh. She raised her eyes to meet the questioning look in Joe's. "*Monsieur*, it would be kind of you to stay," she murmured. "This was going to be my first night alone."

"The storm may last the duration of the night," Joe said softly, watching her reaction to his subtle suggestion that he stay until dawn.

"I know that it would not look decent if you stayed the night," Faye said, clasping her hands nervously together behind her.

"Who the hell cares?" Joe said, hope rising inside him that she was going to allow him to stay...for her protection.

"I do hate to stay alone during this dreadful storm," Faye said, nervously fluttering her eyelashes. "But I do care what people think. If my brother would ever find out that I had asked a man to stay with me, he would perhaps disown me.''

''All your worries will come later,'' Joe argued softly. ''Tonight is the issue, isn't it? You're frightened, and I'm here to see that you no longer have any reason to be. That should be enough.''

He gestured toward her bedroll. ''And you didn't ask me. I came on my own. You go on and lie down and go to sleep,'' he said softly. ''I'll sleep over there by the entrance of the wagon. I'll leave early in the morning before daybreak. No one will be the wiser.'' Except he knew that to be a white lie. The soldiers were close by in their tents, surely envying him.

Faye eyed her unrolled bedroll nervously, then jumped with alarm as thunder roared like a lion overhead. ''All right,'' she quickly agreed, going to her blankets. She pulled a cover up to her chin. ''But you must remove those terribly wet breeches. You can't sleep in them. I don't want to be responsible for you taking pneumonia.''

Joe reached for the lamp and blew the flames out. ''All right,'' he said softly. ''If I must, I must.''

Faye grabbed a spare blanket and tossed it to him, then curled up beneath her own and scarcely breathed as she heard the rustle of clothes. Then a great flash of silver lightning illuminated the muscled sinews of Joe's body. Faye felt her heart skip a beat as she took in his naked form only a few footsteps away from her.

Never had she seen a naked man before, and though the moment had been brief, it had caused a strange ache inside her. A sweet, yet painful ache.

She listened to the movements of his body as he lowered himself to the floor. When another flash of lightning revealed that he was now lying with a blanket drawn over his nudity, Faye's insides calmed.

Turning her back to him, she tried to force her eyes closed so that she could fall asleep, but sleep eluded her. Joe was too close.

She now realized that the feelings his nearness was causing were much more dangerous than any force of nature. She ached for him. If he would approach her at this moment, she knew that she could not deny him.

For the first time in her life she actually wanted a man to teach her the true meaning of being a woman.

Chapter Five

The storm increased its fury. The wagon pitched and rocked as though it were a ship at sea being lashed by high, thunderous waves. Faye huddled beneath her blanket, shivering with fear. When several great crashes of thunder erupted one after the other, she gasped aloud.

Joe raised himself up on an elbow at her soft cry. Through the darkness he looked toward her, and his insides coiled tightly when a flash of lightning revealed her tiny form curled into a tight ball beneath her blanket with the covers drawn over her head.

Dared he go to her and try to comfort her? Would she order him from the wagon if he even tried?

Or had he seen a weakness in her eyes that she would never admit? Though their lips had not touched in the sweet mysteries of a kiss, their eyes had told all.

Daring to chance everything, Joe secured his blanket around his waist.

He moved cautiously to the other end of the wagon and stood over her. Though she was covered by the blanket, he could make out the form of her shapely body.

Dared he proceed? More than once she had looked at him as someone she loathed, yet more often she had looked at him with desire in her eyes.

In one smooth movement, he knelt down beside her. His hands trembling, he reached for the blanket that covered her and gently, very slowly folded it back.

"Faye, don't be frightened," he whispered. "It's me, Joe. I've come to hold you, if you desire it. We can sit the storm out together."

Faye's eyes widened as she watched the blanket being pulled slowly away from her face. Her insides quivered at the sound of Joe's voice, at the gentleness of it.

Wasn't this what she had wanted to see in him since the first time she had realized that she had feelings for him? A gentleness that she had always watched for in a man?

Yet should she trust this side of him? Was it all in pretense to draw her into his arms? Should she trust herself? Only moments ago she had oh, so desired him in the ways of a woman! If she should go to him willingly was she the same as giving him the right to pursue the seduction?

Or was she being foolish by being too suspicious? She was lucky to have found someone to look after her. With Joe there, she was even beginning to feel needed again. But of course this need was much different than that she had experienced with her parents. This need was being drawn from the inner depths of her heart...of her gut. She needed Joe's arms around her. She wanted his lips to devour her! She wanted him to touch her all over and send pleasure soaring through her veins!

A blush heated her cheeks as she felt Joe's eyes on her in the dark. The firm touch of his fingers on her body as he pulled the blanket from her sent flames of passion through her veins. Never had she felt this way before. Joe's wildness seemed to draw something from deep within her.

"Faye?" Joe uttered, smoothing the blanket aside. "Are you sure you want me here? You haven't said a word. Do I frighten you?"

On fire with unleashed rapture, Faye looked up at him, a sudden flash of lightning revealing his sculpted handsomeness to her feasting eyes. Something within her drew her fingers to his face. Slowly she ran them over the hard slope of his jaw, the masculine curve of his chin and then his tightly pressed lips.

His mouth suddenly opened and he drew one of her fingers between his lips. A strange queasiness swept through her when his tongue sucked on her finger, creating the most wondrous sort of sensation between her thighs. Her rapid heartbeat frightened her with its intensity.

"Joe, please...don't..." she murmured, removing her finger from his soft grasp. "This isn't right. It's the storm. It's making me do things that I do not understand. Please...don't..."

The broad expanse of his chest, the fronds of chest hair, and his hardened nipples shone in the glow of silver lightning. Like a moth being drawn to a flame, her hands went to his chest. She twined her fingers through the kinky curls, then splayed her hands across his chest, feeling the knotted hardness of his nipples press into her palms.

"Oh, Joe, I don't want to want you," she said, sighing. "But you do stir me to such passions!"

Joe took one of her hands and kissed its palm gently. "My darling Faye, you seem to draw out the worst in me. And do you know why?"

"No, why?" she whispered shakily, afraid to hear the answer.

"Because I need you," he said huskily. "And I'm tired of fighting my feelings. I sense that you need me, too. Love me, Faye. Let me love you. Let's make it sweet tonight, darling. Let...me...love you."

Faye was momentarily at a loss for words, frightened by the intensity of his spoken feelings for her and of her own for him. If she allowed it, he would seduce her. But surely she was not a woman free for his taking. Wouldn't she hate herself afterward for believing that he cared for her in the way a man should care for a woman? He surely could tell that she was not the sort to give herself willingly to just any man.

Paling at the thought that he would soon discover he was the first, Faye pressed her hands against his chest and scooted away from him. "Joe, perhaps I was wrong to allow this to go this far," she murmured, nervously raking her fingers through her long, streaming hair. "I know nothing of you."

Joe placed his fingers gently about Faye's wrists and drew her close to him, inhaling the sweetness of her hair and skin. He looked down into her eyes, wishing that it were a beautiful, fair day of spring, and that he and Faye were sitting outside under the brightness of the sunlight so that he could look into the depths of her crystal blue eyes.

"Faye, there is not much to know, and I have hidden nothing from you. Now will you allow me to kiss you?" he said huskily, drawing her lips closer. "Then decide what you want of this night. Give it a chance. Give it a chance."

The huskiness of his voice sent Faye's blood rushing from her heart to the juncture of her thighs. *"Oui, s'il vous plaît,"* she whispered, shaken by his nearness, by his ability to make her forget that she had almost hated him just a few hours before.

Nothing would ever feel as beautiful and as right as being kissed by him.

She drifted toward him. When his lips met hers in a gentle, lingering kiss, exquisite sensations spiraled through Faye's body. Her breath quickened as he enfolded her in his solid embrace and kissed her hungrily.

When his hands trailed down her spine to the curve of her buttocks and he drew her up so that she was anchored more firmly against him, she realized that the blanket had slipped away from him. His nudity was boldly pressed against her, with only the thin cotton of her dress between them. Feeling his aroused state drove her to the edge of her own sanity.

Joe's lips left her mouth and he sensuously tasted her closed eyes, her hot cheeks, then the slope of her chin. While he pressed his lips into the delicate column of her neck, his hands deftly unfastened her dress. Faye scarcely breathed when she felt him lowering the bodice over her shoulders, down to her waist until even her hips were bared to him.

A tremor coursed through her at the feel of the cool night air on her skin. She welcomed Joe's arms around her as he lowered her down onto the blankets. She sucked in her breath as his lips sought her breast in the darkness and found it, his tongue flicking about its nipple, causing it to harden to a tight peak.

Joe felt her passion and buried his face in the soft valley of her breasts. He had watched this woman from afar for days, had hungered for her so much that he could hardly bear it. That he was with her now was the fulfillment of his dreams. At his every touch, her body trembled, quivered and grew damp. Without a doubt, her trusting innocence could mean only one thing—she was most surely a virgin. Suddenly his gut twisted and his mouth went dry. He raised his head to again kiss her soft, willing lips, and he took care to caress her gentle curves and her most secret valleys.

"Faye?" he murmured, his fingers now stroking her womanhood, awakening that hidden flower that longed to blossom. "You do want this, don't you?"

Faye's eyes fluttered open and she gazed at him through a cloud of passion. Surely she had been wrong about him all along. At this moment, he was nothing but sweet, gentle and considerate.

Framing his face between her hands, she drew his lips to hers. "Please don't ask questions," she whispered, brushing his lips with her tongue. "Never before have I wanted to be with a man like this. I fear it's because I have fallen in love, Joe. Fallen in love with you."

Joe drew away and looked down at her. He devoured her shadow in the night, then twined his fingers through her hair and drew her lips harshly back to his. He kissed her with a fire and a passion that rendered her weak. She wrapped her arms about his neck, then sought out the sleek lines of his back with her exploring fingers.

Then she reached for the hard lines of his buttocks. Suddenly her breath caught in her throat when Joe took her hand and urged her fingers around his hardness.

With a harsh gasp, his mouth closed hard upon hers, passion flaming his insides as she pleasured him. Blindly, he moved his fingers through the cleft between her thighs. At the warm damp feel of the risen core of her desire, he knew that soon neither of them would be able to wait much longer.

Faye was becoming more and more weakened by building passion. Joe's fingers caressing her in such a way made a stirring within her, as though flames were spreading, searing her. She wanted him. And she could tell by the pulsating of his hardness under her fingers that he wanted her just as much.

She could hardly believe that she was there, so unashamedly touching a man, wanting that part of him to make contact with her.

Joe reached for Faye's hand and eased it away from his hardness. With a lingering look, he straddled her, then very slowly nudged her thighs apart with a knee.

Again he kissed her—a long and sweet kiss. His hands cupped her breasts and kneaded them. Gently he probed his hardness where she was willingly open to receive him. His heart thundered wildly as he finally made the maddening plunge inside her. His kisses smoothed away her momentary cry of pain.

He smiled to himself as deep inside, she relaxed and gave way to pleasure.

The pain between Faye's thighs was ebbed with each gentle thrust that filled her. Locking her legs about his waist, she drew him farther inside her and gave herself to him, mind, body and soul. It was more wonderful than she had ever imagined.

Surely, this was the man she was destined to love forever. This one moment was much too perfect for it to be otherwise. Never could she ever hate or detest Joe Harrison again! There would be only sweet, stolen moments of pleasure between them.

And as for her brother, Michael? He could marry Joe and Faye as soon as they arrived at Fort Smith.

Oui, she would marry the man she was so willingly losing her virginity to as soon as a preacher was available. How perfect it all would be.

Her mind returned to the moment, to the way Joe's strokes within her were speeding up, causing her body to respond in kind. Her heartbeat seemed to be keeping pace as her mind reeled and grew feverish with the building rapture.

Then a sudden current of sweet warmth swept through her, causing her to tremble and cling to Joe as though her very life depended on it. They had reached the magic plateau they had been seeking together. Faye emitted a soft cry of passion that was muffled by a thick, husky groan. Then they both became quiet, breathing hard against the other.

Shaken, she allowed Joe to draw her into the curve of his body and hold her against his warm flesh. She twined her arms about his neck and hugged him, relishing his closeness and the tautness of his muscled body. The wonders of what they had shared together overwhelmed her. Surely no other man could ever make her feel this way. Surely their loving was special, meant for only them to share.

"I can't help but love you," Faye whispered, feeling the pounding of his heart against her body as he held her so tight that she felt as though they were linked together as one being. "Please love me as much."

"I do," Joe whispered, his hands trailing across her silken buttocks. His fingers moved to the wetness between her thighs and resumed caressing her. "Woman, I do love you."

Breathless once more, Faye leaned away from him and stretched across the blankets. Her eyes closed, she gave herself up to the rapture of Joe's lips...first on her breasts, then lower, on the soft skin between her thighs.

Knowing that what he was doing was surely forbidden, Faye fought against asking him not to. She bit her lower lip and tossed her head feverishly from side to side, feeling that same wondrous pleasure as his tongue and lips continued to stroke her.

When her body shook with ecstasy, she welcomed his mouth on her lips, kissing her heatedly as he once again entered her with his newly aroused hardness. Again they sought and found the sensations that had been awakened within them this night.

Chapter Six

The storm had abated, and now only soft raindrops misted the air. Faye eased herself from Joe's arms, sighing. She leaned up on an elbow and looked down at him, able to see only his outline in the darkness. At this moment she would welcome a flash of lightning so that she could devour his handsomeness with her eyes.

She was so strangely at peace with herself. It was the first time for such serenity since her parents' deaths, and she could hardly believe that Joe Harrison was the cause. Never would she have thought that a man could steal her heart away so easily and that she would so willingly give herself to him.

Surely Joe Harrison would never again ignite such angry sparks inside her. Forevermore, she would idolize him.

"What are you thinking?" Joe asked, interrupting her thoughts, his hand reaching to mold one of her breasts within its callused palm.

Faye's breath was taken by his thumb circling her hardened nipple. She swallowed hard as she guided his hand away and moved to fit her body into the curve of his side.

"I am thinking so many things at this moment," she said, laying an arm across his broad chest. "I haven't been so content in a long time. The deaths of my parents sent me into such depths of despair, and then the realization that I must leave New Orleans to travel to the wilderness made the trauma in my life twofold."

She moved to a sitting position and drew a blanket around her shoulders. "And then there were those terrible moments when you and I were constantly at each other's throat," she said, drawing her knees up to hug them. "Sometimes I swear I could have knocked you in the head."

"I guess I would have deserved it," Joe said, reaching in the dark to twine his fingers through her hair. He drew her mouth to his. "I'm glad you spared me such a wound."

Faye trembled as his lips brushed across her mouth in a sweet and tender kiss. "I love you so," she whispered. "I don't want to lose what we found together tonight, especially over a stupid misunderstanding. It would be devastating now that we have shared so much within one another's arms."

Joe kneaded her breast beneath her blanket and a familiar warmth spread within him at the touch of her. "I will try to be more patient," he said softly. "But sometimes it seems that my patience runs thin. Especially with women."

Faye leaned away from him. "But why, Joe?" she asked, her breath catching as his hand moved lower and his fingers caressed her abdomen. "What is it about women that makes you not want to trust me?"

Joe moved away from her. Though he had confessed to loving her, he still could not reveal his deepest hurts and feelings. Who was to say that in the near future she would not run scared back to the city and leave him empty and angry all over again? She was going to have to prove herself to him before he would confide in her about anything. Making love with him was not proof of her good intentions. It would take much more than that for him to truly trust her.

"Joe," she said uneasily, reaching for his hand, clasping it. "I have already told you about my parents' deaths and why I was traveling to Fort Smith. I even explained how hard this is on me."

She swallowed, then eased into his arms and hugged him tightly to her. The blanket had dropped away from her and their bare chests met. "Joe, I'm afraid," she murmured. "I'm not sure if I can adjust to living in the wilderness. I so adored city life. I miss my friends! What if I can't accept the loneliness of the wilderness?"

Joe stiffened against her, and guided her away from him. If she doubted herself so much, how could he trust her?

Faye was stunned by his sudden coldness. Again she had said something wrong to him! But what? She had only been searching for his sympathy and comfort.

"Joe, what is it?" she murmured. She grabbed a blanket about her shoulders and scurried to her feet. "What did I say? Don't you see what I was doing? I wanted you to tell me that I was wrong...that I could adjust. I was going to ask you to help me."

She searched for him in the darkness, moving in the direction of the rustling of his clothes as he stepped into them. When she found him, she grabbed his arm. "Don't leave me like this," she pleaded softly. "Say something. Joe, I feel so suddenly empty. Don't be the one to cause this inside me. I gave myself to you tonight. I trusted you!"

His heart pounded at the sound of her pleadings, yet he knew that what was between them was futile. He placed his hands on her arms and looked down into her face. "Faye, it's no longer storming," he said flatly. "I am no longer needed here. You will be all right by yourself. It's my duty to go and check the river depth. It will be left up to me and Bart to decide whether or not the wagon train proceeds tomorrow or is delayed because of swollen waters. Do you understand? I really must go."

Shaken by his sudden coolness, Faye could not speak for a moment. She did not want him to hear the quavering in her voice. Only moments before she had been the happiest woman in the world. She had been held in the arms of the man she loved! He had said that he loved her!

And now she was left with only an ugly memory, for Joe had not been sincere.

"Then go," she finally managed to say. "No one is stopping you. I certainly won't. I have nothing else to say to you now or ever." She flailed a hand in the air. *"Bon soir, monsieur!"*

She jerked away from him then, grabbing the blanket as it threatened to fall away from her. She would never let him see her naked again! He would never so much as touch her again, for she knew when she had been taken advantage of.

Pausing for a moment, he tried to see Faye through the darkness, aching to draw her into his arms and to tell her that he was sorry. Then, reining in his emotions, Joe spun around and climbed from the wagon. He cursed beneath his breath when his moccasined feet sank into mud. Making his way across the rain-soaked ground, he stormed toward the river.

Bitter tears streamed down Faye's cheeks. She flung herself onto her pallet of blankets, pummeling her fists into the bedroll as she cursed the day she had laid eyes on Joe Harrison. Her heart was breaking into a million pieces, for she now knew that he had used her. How could she have been so foolish? So blind? Her body was still alive from his caresses, her heart torn in two by his love and his hate.

Sobbing into her pillow, she fell into a fitful sleep.

In what seemed like minutes later, she was awakened with a start when the wagonmaster shouted a warning to everyone that it was time to get ready to start on the journey again.

With daylight barely lighting the interior of the wagon, Faye rose up on one elbow and rubbed her tear-swollen eyes. She looked at her clothes strewn along the floor of the wagon and then down at her body as she brushed a blanket aside. The shameful reminders that she had been with a man intimately for the first time in her life seemed to be evident everywhere she looked. Would she even be able to hold her chin up with pride again?

"Oh! How I hate him!" she remarked hotly, combing her fingers angrily through her tousled hair. With that the aroma of coffee and simmering beans made Faye's stomach growl. It was time to begin a new day, one that was bound to be long and arduous.

Opening her trunk of clothes, Faye chose a simple cotton dress and fresh underthings and slipped into them. Wary of the mud, she yanked on knee-high leather boots. Her tangled hair pulled her scalp as she anxiously brushed it.

Determined to face the day with strong will, Faye threw open the flap and climbed from the wagon. She winced when her boots sank into the mud, and her insides grew numb with a desire she did not want to feel when she heard Joe's voice not all that far from where she stood. He was arguing with the wagonmaster, stating that it was imperative that the caravan get on its way. If they let risen waters stop them every time it rained, they would never reach Fort Smith.

Faye turned her eyes slowly to Joe. His face was red, and his eyes flashed with anger. He gestured toward the river as he talked, his words clipped.

"You didn't hire me and Bart just to protect you against outlaws and the sort," Joe half shouted. "You also hired us for our opinion, and I say it *is* all right to get on our way this morning. There are ways to cross the river even when it's overflowing its banks. Now do we do it or stay here like cowards?"

Faye paled, hearing the note of desperation in Joe's voice. No one else seemed enthusiastic about pushing on. It was obvious that Joe was alone in this conviction.

She turned her eyes away from him, not wanting to admit that he was eager to reach Fort Smith so that he could be rid of her. Looking toward the sky, she no longer saw signs of rain. The sky was blue, the sun just now rising and washing the bluffs in a pale gold light. Flocks of passenger pigeons passed overhead, and the forest was alive with the chirping and singing of birds.

But those pleasant sounds were almost drowned out by the great, thunderous rush of the Arkansas River.

Faye's heart pounded erratically at the thought of having to drive the oxen and wagon through the raging water. If only Gayland was well enough to take charge again.

In an attempt to strengthen her resolve, Faye lifted the skirt of her dress and joined the other women and men beside the fire. Her hopes rose when she saw Celia dishing out beans onto two tin platters. If Gayland was well enough to eat, perhaps he could return to his wagon.

The mud sucking at her boots, Faye made her way over to Celia and softly touched her arm. "Celia, how is Gayland?" she asked, her eyes anxious.

Celia looked pale and drawn as she eased a plate of beans into Faye's hand. "Gayland is no better," she murmured. "Here. Eat, honey. We don't have much time. For some reason Joe Harrison is anxious to move on. I went ahead and prepared a breakfast for you since you were still sleeping. I know how it must tax you to be in charge of everything. I apologize for that, Faye. Perhaps in a few days it will all change for the better."

Faye frowned as she looked down at the plate of beans, then back up into Celia's eyes. Her hopes of reprieve were dashed. The food had not been for Gayland at all.

"I'm sorry Gayland is still ailing," Faye said, accepting a fork as Celia handed it to her.

"Again I apologize," Celia said softly. She studied Faye's eyes. "Honey, I now know you so well. I can tell when something is wrong. Have you been crying? I worried about you during the storm, but I couldn't leave Gayland. His temperature had risen, and I needed to bathe him with cold compresses. Was it all so terrible for you, honey?"

Faye ducked her head and began scooping beans into her mouth. She had had no idea that her distress was so evident.

"Faye, what is it?" Celia asked, placing a finger to Faye's chin and lifting it so their eyes could meet and hold. "Something did happen last night."

Feeling a blush rising to her cheeks, Faye forced a soft laugh. "It was only the storm," she murmured. "I hate them so. The lightning was fierce, wasn't it?"

Celia tilted her head. "Yes, it was fierce," she murmured. "Next time I will be sure to see that you are not alone."

Faye's eyes wavered. Again she forced a smile, then looked over her shoulder at Joe, who was now talking with Bart Dobbs only a few feet away from her. His voice carried on the wind, each syllable reminding her of her shame.

"I believe I can weather future storms alone just fine, Celia," she said dryly. "I came through the ordeals of last night just fine."

Chapter Seven

"Stretch out!"

At the command of the wagonmaster, each wagon began to fall into its appointed place, and with a universal cracking of whips the march began toward the river.

Wearing soft leather gloves, Faye clung to the reins and watched her two oxen begin their slow, lumbering walk. Never in her life had she been so tense. The pit of her stomach was queasy and her mouth was dry, the responsibility of being in charge of Gayland's wagon weighing heavily on her shoulders.

She swallowed hard as she peered ahead and saw the river just beyond a long row of cottonwood trees. Its banks overflowing, she could see the water churning, carrying with it all sorts of debris.

Faye caught sight of Joe and Bart as they rode at a fast gallop toward the river. When they arrived there, she watched Joe's expression as he studied the water. He kneaded his chin nervously while exchanging comments with Bart and giving the river occasional troubled glances.

"Surely he will change his mind," Faye whispered. "The river is much too treacherous to cross!"

Joe slipped from his horse to the ground, leaving his reins looped around the saddle horn. She watched him as he nervously paced beside the river. In his buckskin attire, his muscles were corded at his shoulders, his chest was broad and his thighs tapered. Bronzed from the relentless sun, his face belonged to the gods.

She would never forget the rapturous moments with him alone in the wagon. It tore at her heart to know that he had used her, then left her alone. His profession of love had sounded so sincere; he had made love to her with such gentle sweetness....

Suddenly her every nerve ending tightened when she saw Joe motion with a hand for the wagons to proceed toward the river. No matter how fierce the waters appeared, he deemed it necessary for the journey to continue.

She craned her neck to see how the first wagon fared in the treacherous waters. Then as the wagons traveling ahead of her stopped, she stopped hers. Her eyes widened in surprise when she saw that one by one the wagons were now being fastened together with ropes and chains. When Joe came by foot to Faye's wagon, they exchanged bitter, sour glances.

"I know you are wondering why we're doing this," Joe said, finally breaking the silence. "The riverbank is muddy and soft. It's safer to attach all the wagons in case one of them gets stuck. The other teams can help pull it out."

"Thank you, *monsieur*, for enlightening me," Faye said sarcastically. "Now I feel much better about the task at hand."

Joe gave her a perturbed look as he fastened the last chain while Bart tied a rope to the other side of the wagon. "You'll be just fine," he said, straightening his long, lean legs and placing his hands on his hips. "Just you follow the lead and do what everyone else does."

He looked away for a moment, and he ran a hand down his cheek. "Perhaps I had better take charge of your wagon," he said hoarsely. "At least until you get safely across the river. Bart can handle things up front."

Faye took a deep breath, for a moment believing that he still cared and that she had only imagined his ill feelings. It would be easy to accept his gesture of kindness, but she saw it as only that. A gesture of kindness that he would offer to any woman in distress. Nothing more!

"*Merci*, but no, that won't be necessary," she said stiffly. "Just go on about your duties. I can see to my own. As I see it, crossing the river will be as simple as pie."

She hoped that he did not see the nervous perspiration beading her brow at the thought of having to handle the wagon and team of oxen alone. But never would she stoop so low as to accept Joe Harrison's assistance for anything again.

Joe shrugged with indifference. "Sounds like you've got a handle on everything, all right," he said smoothly, and turned and walked away from her. Once he reached the lead wagon, he stood off to the side and shouted orders as a whip cracked and the oxen ploughed into the churning, cold waters.

Faye began to tremble as her wagon gave a sudden lurch and then moved roughly along with the others through the deep furrows in the muddy trail. She held her breath as more oxen and more wagons headed for the water. The oxen bellowed and snorted in terror, and the incessant cracks of the whips sounded over the rush of the water.

Faye's attention was drawn to her own oxen as they balked and stubbornly pulled at their bits. At their refusal to move, the ropes and chains that attached her to the rest of the wagons groaned under the strain. Without hesitating, Faye raised her arm and brought the whip cracking down across their backs. With a sudden jolt, the wagon moved forward.

Her fingers trembling and her stomach queasy with fear, Faye watched the river draw closer and closer. As her own team of oxen splashed into the

water, their heads bobbed beneath the surface.
Faye's eyes widened with fear for the next moment
until they reappeared, then she breathed a deep sigh
of relief as the oxen snorted and sputtered in a wild
attempt to keep their heads above water.

Faye clung tightly to the reins and balanced herself as the wagon began to pitch and lurch, the current threatening to topple it over.

A grating, thunderous snap sounded from beneath the boards of her seat. Faye's heart felt as
though it had plummeted to her feet when she realized that the chain that fastened her wagon to the
others had broken. With the sudden jerking of the
wagon, she lost her balance.

"Oh, non!" she screamed, forced to let go of the
reins. *"Mon Dieu! A l'aide!* Help!''

When she fell into the water, she felt herself being
tossed about as though she were a mere leaf. She
gulped for air, then was pulled below the surface as
the water thundered over her head. Bobbing in the
water, she searched around her wildly as the current
carried her with it. Tangled branches swirled past
her, and she grasped for them but was not successful.

Again she was sucked beneath the water until her
lungs began to ache.

Suddenly strong hands were on her waist, drawing her up to the surface. Fighting for air, her hair
wet and heavy over her face, Faye coughed and

spewed. She clung to the solidly muscled arms of her rescuer as he carried her to the shore.

Opening her eyes, she groaned to herself. Of all the men in the caravan, why did Joe Harrison always have to be there when she was in trouble? It was as though fate always led him to her.

Chilled to the bone, Faye had no choice but to hold tight to Joe as he carried her up the slippery banks of the river where all other wagons but hers had forded without a mishap. She looked over her shoulder as Bart was just now guiding her wagon on up to the shore, the rope that had been secured on the one side having held after the chain had broken.

Shivering, her teeth rattling, Faye felt faint. Her legs barely held her up when Joe placed her on her feet close enough to her wagon that she could see that it had come through the ordeal unharmed. She wove her fingers through her wet and tangled hair as she looked down at herself. Embarrassed, she could see how the wet dress defined the hardened nipples of her breasts.

Hugging her arms across her chest, she slowly raised her eyes. Joe was giving her a look that she understood too well. He wasn't openly chiding her for not being able to keep control of things, but his smug expression said it all.

Her eyes snapping, Faye glared at him. "It's all your fault," she accused. "You knew the dangers of crossing the river. You're just lucky mine was the only mishap.''

"I offered to take charge of your wagon," Joe said blandly. "Can I help it if you were foolish enough to decline?''

"You are not the sort to admit to being wrong, are you?'' Faye continued, a puddle forming at her feet. "You won't admit that one more day beside the river would have been best."

"As I see it, I wasn't wrong," Joe said tightly. "The wagons are all safe and ready to proceed. Even your wagon is safe." A slow smile lifted his lips. "Even you are among the living, Faye, thanks to me."

"If you think I will thank you for dragging me out of the river, you are fooling yourself," Faye said, taking a step away from him. "I shouldn't have been there in the first place."

"No, you shouldn't have been there," Joe growled. "If I had anything to do with it, this never would have happened." He motioned with a hand. "Go on. Get aboard. Get inside your wagon and get into something dry and warm. I will take charge of the wagon the rest of the way to Fort Smith or until Gayland can resume his duties."

"You can forget that!" Faye retorted angrily. She turned with a jerk and walked heatedly toward her wagon. "I will not allow you anywhere near my wagon again.''

"Oh? And you wish to continue on the trip dressed in wet clothes?" Joe chided her.

Faye's footsteps faltered. She turned slowly and faced him. "No, I don't think so," she murmured. "Please allow me enough time to change before getting the caravan on its way again."

Joe sauntered away from her. "I think I can manage that," he said, nodding at Bart, who was climbing down from Faye's wagon. "Come on, Bart. I think we've used up our usefulness here. The lady thinks she can handle things on her own again. I guess we can't argue with a lady, now can we?"

Shivering, Faye watched Joe and Bart walk away from her. It took everything in her not to call to Joe and tell him that she was wrong, that she did not wish to have the responsibilities of the wagon. But never again did she want his favors.

"Faye!"

With a start, Faye turned, then welcomed Celia into her arms as she hugged the small woman fitfully to her.

"I just heard!" Celia cried. "Oh, Faye, I feel so responsible! If only Gayland was well!"

Faye clung to Celia. "But he isn't all right, and you must return to his side," she reassured her friend. "What just happened is unfortunate, but it's over and I am all right. Please go back to Gayland. I'll be more careful, Celia. Nothing like this will happen again. You'll see."

Celia disengaged herself from Faye's embrace and began walking her to their wagon. "You get on into the wagon and get changed into something dry, and I'll ride with you for a short while today," she said firmly. "Doc Rose says Gayland doesn't need me so much anymore. His temperature has broken somewhat."

Faye looked quickly over at Celia. "Does that mean that he will be able to return to the wagon?"

"Not yet," Celia said softly. "What he has is still highly contagious. We certainly don't want you to come down with it."

Faye's knees were weak as she pulled herself inside the wagon, Celia close behind her. "But what about yourself?" she said, grabbing a towel and wrapping it about her wet hair.

"A wife's place is beside her husband," Celia said, sorting through Faye's trunk, taking a cotton dress and underthings from inside it. She placed them aside and rose to her feet to help Faye remove her wet, clinging clothes. "One day you'll see. There will be a special man for you. You'll be ready to give your life for him the same as I would for Gayland. There's such a special bond that is formed between a man and woman in love."

Faye gave Celia an uneasy glance. "Yes, perhaps one day," she murmured, slipping her dress over her head. At the sound of Joe's voice just on the other side of the canvas, her stomach tightened.

"Faye, we can't take much longer," he warned. "We've got to get on our way. There are many miles ahead of us. No need in wasting any more time."

Celia looked at Faye as she picked Faye's wet clothes up from the floor. "That man is sure anxious to arrive at Fort Smith," she said, then nodded knowingly. "But of course he must have a woman waiting there for him."

Chapter Eight

The caravan of wagons first ambled across a flat plane, then wound its way through rugged mountains. They passed over springs and sparkling streams that coursed down the timbered ridges. The rough terrain made for arduous travel, and Faye was glad when flat land was reached again. The fear of her oxen-drawn wagon slipping off the narrow mountain passes had become worse than her fear of storms.

Celia had returned to Doc Rose's wagon to minister to Gayland, and Faye once again felt the heavy burden of her loneliness. Clutching the reins, her backside sore from the long ride on the hard wagon seat, she tried to focus her attention on her surroundings. It was a lovely spring afternoon. Redbud trees grew in breathtaking purple masses, and the dogwood trees were in full bloom.

Faye grimaced when she noticed that the trail was becoming more difficult. Although the rains had stopped and the rivers had receded, the deep furrows carved by the previous wagons were filled with water. As her wagon wheels jounced in and out of the holes, her body jerked and swayed, and her temples began to pound unmercifully.

Nervously nibbling on her lower lip, she became aware of the taste of salt and perspiration and dust. Knowing that she must be a sight, she groaned out loud.

Faye turned her eyes from her mud-splattered skirt and callused hands, only to find Joe's eyes leveled at her as he silently studied her stooped form. Lifting her chin haughtily, she stared straight ahead and stubbornly pretended that the lurch of the wagon as the wheels dropped into yet another pothole didn't bother her in the slightest.

Then her eyes widened and her breath caught in her throat when she heard the splintering of wood and a prolonged creak. She screamed when one end dropped clumsily as a wheel became disengaged and began to roll across the land.

Faye grabbed the seat to keep from being thrown by the wagon's thrust as one end dropped precariously to the ground. Stunned, Faye sat and watched the wheel come to rest in a thick bed of grass.

Blowing at a stray strand of hair, Faye climbed resignedly from the wagon, and with her hands on her hips and her legs spread, stood and stared down at the damaged wagon.

The sound of a horse approaching made her grow tense. She closed her eyes and clenched her teeth, knowing who it was before looking up or hearing his voice.

"I got it, Joe!" Bart shouted.

Faye's cheeks warmed with a blush when Bart reached her side, smiling toothily, his dark eyes brimming with friendliness. She smiled awkwardly back at him, then grimaced at his teasing wink.

"Seems you lost something, ma'am," he said, rolling the wheel toward the crippled wagon and letting it drop to the ground beside it. "Can't make much progress on the trail without four healthy wheels, now can you?"

Out of the corner of her eye Faye saw Joe swing himself out of his saddle and begin to lumber toward her, his dark hair windblown. She scooted past Bart, desperate to be able to repair the wagon herself. Lifting the hem of her dress, Faye knelt on one knee and moaned to herself when she felt the mud soak into her dress and on through her petticoat to her bare knee. With her gloved hands she picked up the wheel and leaned it up against the wagon, studying it, trying to understand how it had come loose and how it might be replaced.

"Step aside," Joe commanded as he moved beside her. "I don't think you've noticed that you're being left behind. If Bart and I don't get busy repairing the wagon now, it will take several cracks of the whip on the oxen's backs to catch up with the others."

At Joe's brisk order, Faye jerked to her feet. She glared at him, her eyes afire with anger, knowing that she had no choice but to yield to this man. Silently, she folded her arms across her chest and backed away as the two men set about the task at hand.

The pounding and hammering and the grunts and groans of the two men hard at work made Faye feel contrite. How foolish of her to think that she could have replaced the wheel herself. Already Joe had removed his shirt and his back was sleek with perspiration, his body taking on a golden sheen beneath the brightness of the midafternoon sun.

Taken by his handsomeness and his vibrant masculinity, Faye swung around to face away from him. She swallowed hard as her heart thundered inside her. No matter how much Joe's silent cold behavior was hurting her, she knew that she loved him too much not to want him in her arms again.

"As good as new," she heard him say as he moved toward her.

When she turned and their eyes met and held, she set her jaw firmly and steadied herself beneath his steady, searching gaze. She recognized something in his eyes that she had seen before. He was looking at her with a keen gentleness, the same sort of look that he had given her just prior to the moment when he had drawn her into his arms.

At just that moment Bart Dobbs stepped aside to let Faye climb aboard. She gave the wagon a quick once-over, then looked at Bart before stepping on the lower step of the wagon. There was something about his quiet friendliness that she could not ignore.

"I truly do appreciate what you've done," she murmured. "*Merci*, Bart."

"It was my pleasure, ma'am," Bart said, nodding. He started to place a hand on Faye's elbow to assist her into the wagon, but when she jerked away from him, he reconsidered.

Chuckling low, he walked toward Joe and stood with him, watching Faye as she settled down into the wagon. A nasty crack of the whip, and the oxen were once more ambling along the muddy trail.

"Take it easy, Faye!" Bart shouted. "We wouldn't want you losin' any more wheels, or anything else, for that matter!"

Joe gave Bart a dirty look. Faye stiffened.

Faye sat beside Celia and finished off a plate of corn pone that had been prepared with small pieces of buffalo meat in the hot ashes of the campfire. The sun brimmed the horizon, and the air was filled with the pleasant scent of boiled coffee and simmering beans.

Faye looked down at her soiled skirt, then toward the forest, where not far beyond its dense cover was a meandering stream. She gave Celia a pensive stare, then looked down at the rifle and change of clothes beside her.

"You really don't mind accompanying me to the stream to keep watch while I take a quick bath?" she asked softly, spying Joe's broad shoulders from across the fire and hoping he hadn't heard.

A fiddle was being tuned somewhere close by. There had been talk of having a dance after everyone had finished their evening meal. It was a beautifully warm night, and hopes were high. After they had left the troubled waters of the Arkansas River behind, many miles had been traveled. Everyone was praising Joe for his prowess as a scout. In their eyes he could do no wrong.

Celia shivered involuntarily as she glanced down at the rifle. "I do so hate firearms," she murmured, her green eyes squinting as she looked toward the forest.

Faye laughed nervously. "Let's just go and get it over with. I feel as though I have dust from the tip of my toes to my head. And the mud? At least most of it is on my skirt instead of me."

Celia looked sadly at Doc Rose's wagon. "It will be still a few days before Gayland is strong enough to take charge of our wagon again," she said. Her eyes lit up as she looked back at Faye. "But, Faye, at least he should be able to return tomorrow. Isn't that just grand?"

Faye leaned over and hugged Celia. "Yes, that's grand," she said, her insides warmed with the news. "I've missed you both so much."

Celia patted Faye's back. "Let's go and get your bath over with," she encouraged. "As the sun lowers in the sky, the temperatures become way too cool for bathing, and it is more dangerous in the woods at dusk. Some animals wait for dark to search for prey."

Faye's eyes were drawn to Joe as she eased from Celia's gentle embrace. Her heart beat erratically when their eyes met. "Yes, I know," she whispered. "All sorts of animals wait for dusk."

Grabbing her change of clothes and a towel, Faye hesitated to leave when Joe still watched her, but as long as Celia was with her, he would not dare come anywhere near where she planned to bathe.

Her chin held high, she walked beside Celia into the thick brush, then looked at Celia to make sure she had the rifle. She did. Her fingers were clutched about its barrel so tightly her knuckles were white.

Smiling, Faye pushed her way onward, the water of the stream ahead sparkling like diamonds in the crisp, evening light.

Chapter Nine

The gravel-filled creek meandered through intermittent deep pools and shallow water. Her petticoat clinging to her, Faye stood knee-deep in the water, splashing her shoulders to rinse the soap from them. She was keeping her eye on a sleek, agile otter just upstream, then looked upward at a red-shouldered hawk soaring overhead.

"Hurry up," Celia fussed from the banks of the creek. "I'm frightened, Faye."

Knowing that darkness was near, Faye lowered herself to her knees and dipped her hair into the water. Furiously scrubbing soap into it she ignored Celia's pleadings. She, too, understood the dangers of lingering too long away from the campsite.

Celia paced back and forth, her fingers trembling. She looked nervously around her, and her breath caught in her throat when she heard the crunch of leaves and the breaking of twigs from somewhere close by.

"Faye, did you hear that?" she asked, stopping to peer more intensely into the brush. "Faye, did you?"

Celia looked toward her and saw that her head was momentarily ducked beneath the water to rinse out the soap.

A low, menacing growl rumbled through the forest. Celia's eyes widened, aware of the black bears that roamed the bottomland. Taking a careful step backward, numb with fear, she dropped the rifle and turned and began running blindly away. When she reached the campsite and ran bodily into Joe, she looked up at him, panic-stricken.

"Faye!" she gasped, breathless. "She's in the creek bathing, and I heard a bear. You must go to her rescue." She placed a hand to her throat as she looked in the direction of the creek. "Please hurry. She's depending on me to keep watch, and I panicked and ran. I even dropped my rifle. Please go to her and make sure she's safe."

Joe looked past Celia into the forest. "But if Faye is bathing," he said hoarsely, "she would not appreciate my presence."

"Good Lord, Joe," Celia said, her voice rising. "She cannot object if you have come to save her from a bear."

"I do believe she has grown tired of my rescues," Joe grumbled, bending to pick up his rifle. "But if I must, I must."

Celia grabbed his arm. "Don't let anything happen to her," she pleaded. "She's become special to me and Gayland."

"I can see that she has," Joe said, smiling down at Celia. He eased her hand from his arm. "And don't you worry about a thing. If there is a bear anywhere close to Faye, I'll see to it that she is not harmed."

Placing a hand over her mouth, Celia watched Joe head into the forest, his rifle primed and ready.

Joe moved stealthily through the forest, his eyes trained to catch the movement of an animal no matter what its size. And a bear would not be hard to spy. But thus far there were no signs of a bear. He had not even heard a growl. If Celia's imagination had not been playing tricks on her and she had heard the bear, it had taken off in another direction.

This left Joe in a predicament of sorts. He could not leave Faye bathing without someone standing guard, and she most certainly would not approve of his being there.

Creeping on through the tangled brush, Joe heard the splash of water just ahead and tensed. The only thing to do was to get close enough so that he could listen for sounds of trouble, yet not so close that he could actually see her. Then she would have no reason to accuse him of anything indecent, though every part of him wanted to take a look at her and see her wet and naked body. It took all the willpower that he could muster not to join her in the water and draw her into his arms and make love to her until she begged for more.

Clearing his throat nervously, Joe knelt down behind the thick trunk of an oak tree and disciplined his eyes straight ahead. He plucked a blade of grass and thrust it between his teeth, his loins aching.

He leaned back and switched his rifle from one hand to the other, his blood boiling with desire. Yet he kept his eyes leveled ahead of him.

With each and every splash of the water, he flinched, his willpower weakening.

Faye wrung her hair out, loving the feel of the water on her clean flesh, and turned to head back to the bank. Peering through the dim light, she squinted, searching for Celia's small frame where she had seen her last. She craned her neck and looked desperately along the banks of the creek. Panic suddenly rose inside her like bolts of lightning. "Celia?" she cried. "Where are you?"

When there was no reply, she stood in the water a moment longer. It did not take much common sense to realize that Celia had deserted her post. But why? Had something frightened her?

Her knees weak with fright, Faye moved from the pebbled creekbed. Water pooled at her feet as she wrapped her towel around her, shivering. Her petticoat was cold and clung to her hips and thighs. She was afraid to move, and her eyes were wide with fright.

An object in the grass just ahead caught Faye's eye. She peered intensely at it and discovered the rifle that Celia had been carrying.

"No!" she gasped.

Dropping the towel to the ground, she rushed to the rifle and picked it up. She positioned it in front of her and stood her ground waiting....

Joe spun on his heel when he heard Faye cry out for Celia. He was just about to respond when Bart came swaggering along, tipping a bottle of whiskey to his lips. His insides rippled cold as Bart spied him standing beside the tree and eased the bottle down.

"Well, hi there, partner," Bart said loudly, hiccuping as he teetered on toward Joe. "What are you doing out here all alone? I came to take a splash in the creek. Don't you think I need sobering up?"

"Oh, no," Joe groaned, knowing that most surely Faye had heard. He turned slowly around and looked through the brush, this time forgetting his earlier hesitation.

His insides coiled tightly when he saw her standing with a rifle lifted, ready to shoot. But it was not so much the rifle that drew his attention. It was the way her petticoat was clinging to her perfect body, her breasts so magnificently outlined, and her flat tummy leading his eyes downward.

Standing there so vulnerably, she was like a beacon beckoning to him.

Faye gasped with alarm when she heard Bart Dobbs so close, heard him talking to Joe. Most surely they had been spying on her while she had been taking her bath.

Feeling the heat of a blush rush to her cheeks, Faye dropped the rifle and folded her arms protectively over her breasts, yet knew it wasn't enough to hide herself from hungry eyes. Her petticoat was clinging to her, revealing her every curve and dip.

"Eh, bien!" Faye yelled into the thick vegetation of the forest. "I know you're there. Are you too cowardly to show yourselves?"

Not at all amused by Faye's accusation, Joe stepped out into full view and began taking long strides toward her. "So you think that I would stoop so low as to sneak about to watch you take a bath?" he stormed. He walked on past Faye and picked up her towel and angrily placed it around her shoulders. "Woman, I've better things to do with my time."

Just then Bart stepped into the clearing and lumbered toward her, teetering as he clutched his whiskey bottle. It did not take much to see that he was drunk.

"How's it goin', ma'am?" Bart asked, chuckling beneath his breath. His gaze raked over her. "Why, you beat me to the creek. I was comin' to take a bath, and guess who I wandered into?" He went to Joe and swung an arm around his shoulder. "My good ol' buddy Joe here." He squinted as he looked up at the long-haired scout. "Joe, you never said. Why are you here?"

Suddenly a light sparked in the drunken scout's eye as he looked Faye over, his gaze stopping at her feet. There, in plain view, lay the rifle. "Well I'll be damned!" He winked at her playfully. "Are you takin' potshots at our ace sharpshooter here— *again*?" At the sharp looks Joe and Faye exchanged, he laughed even louder. "I reckon I'm not the only one who heard that blast…. Sure didn't stop ol' Joe, though, did it?" At that, he placed his face closer to Faye and sniffed. "My but she does smell pretty, even if she does tote a gun," he said, steadying himself against Joe. "Think I can smell as pretty?"

Joe clasped Bart's shoulders and began guiding him to the creek. "Bart, I think you're going to smell like whiskey all night unless I do this," he said, giving Bart a shove. Then he stood back and watched his friend topple clumsily into the water.

Bart shouted and cursed as he splashed about, losing his balance but managing to hang on to the whiskey bottle. He began laughing boisterously as he looked up at Joe. "Come in and join me," he said, gesturing with a hand. "You'll smell sweet, too, Joe."

Faye stood with her mouth agape, clutching the towel around her. She looked from Joe to Bart, then quickly composed herself as Joe turned to look her square in the eye.

"Now you listen to me good," he growled. "I wasn't watching you take a bath. Nor was Bart. I was back at the camp minding my own business when Celia came running to me saying something about a bear. She said that you were bathing and she was supposed to have been keeping watch for you. Dammit, Faye, I could've left you here all alone and wouldn't have had to take this tongue-lashing of yours. But I had to make sure that you were all right."

"And while doing so you took full advantage," she said, pouting. "Thank goodness I hadn't taken off all my clothes. You would have really gotten an eyeful then, wouldn't you?"

Joe leaned his face down to hers and spoke so low that only she could hear. "It's not as though I've never seen you without your clothes on before," Joe said tightly. "Or do you forget all that easily?"

Faye swallowed hard. "That was all a mistake, and you know it," she said dryly. "And just because you did see me undressed once does not give you license to see me that way again."

"Are you saying that you would say no if I asked you to make love again?" Joe asked.

"What?" Faye gasped. She drew the towel more snugly around her shoulders. "Joe Harrison, you have some nerve asking me that. If I recall accurately, you were the one who decided to sever our relationship, a relationship that had gotten out of hand. And just what drew you away from me so quickly?"

"I had my duties to attend to."

"Well, they most certainly weren't to me."

"It might have appeared that way. But if you recall, we had just had one hell of a storm. I had to check the river depths."

"And even though you found it treacherous, you chose to send the caravan on through, anyway."

Joe cast his eyes downward, evading her implied question. Leaning down, he said, "You'll be needing these," and with that he thrust her clothes into her free hand. Faye looked up at him, torn with feelings for him. "*Merci*," she murmured, clutching the clothes to her chest. She looked past him to Bart, who was climbing from the creek, shaking water from his hair. "I do need to change into these. Could you keep watch so I can change into them in privacy?"

"Before you were ready to curse me for keeping watch," Joe said, searching her face, seeing that her mood was softening.

"That was before," she said quietly. "Things are different now."

She looked and found a protective covering of bushes and started to walk toward it, but Joe hurried to her and stopped her again. He held out her rifle. "You also forgot this," he said. "Though I'll be keeping watch, it's best that you have this with you, anyway. No sense in taking chances."

"No," she said, smiling awkwardly up at him. "No sense at all."

Faye turned and went to stand behind a cluster of lilac bushes dripping with fragrant purple flowers and hurriedly pulled on her clothes. She so wanted to be glad that some sort of sanity had been restored between her and Joe, yet she couldn't let herself trust him enough to become the sort of friends they had become in the brief time it had taken to make love. She was learning there were many ways to be foolish. To fall for Joe Harrison would be her most foolish mistake ever.

Fully dressed, Faye stepped from behind the lilac bushes and walked on past Joe, who was steadying Bart as they walked toward the campsite. Faye rushed on ahead to the square dance that was now in full swing. The fiddler was playing a snappy, merry tune while feet stomped and skirts whirled.

Faye looked at Joe over her shoulder as he came into camp. The golden campfire was reflected in his dark eyes.

Chapter Ten

Tapping her toe in rhythm with the music, Faye stood outside the wide circle of dancers, watching as the first couples saluted, then swung around, curtsied and changed partners. She was quickly becoming familiar with such calls as promenade, form a star, grand right and left, swing your partner, and ladies chain.

"Do-si-do!" the caller shouted above the constant squawking of the fiddle. "Swing her high! Swing her low! Don't step on her pretty toe!"

Faye was so taken with the gaiety of the moment that she didn't hear Joe move to her side. For a while she had forgotten him and his disturbing ways.

But when his voice spoke so close beside her, his breath hot on her ear, she was catapulted back into that abyss of sensual forebodings.

"Would you like to dance?" Joe asked, daring to slip an arm around her waist.

Faye gazed slowly up into his dark, fathomless eyes. "I doubt if I will ever understand you," she said dryly. "First you act as though I am the plague and can't get away from me fast enough, and now you are friendly again, as though you never treated me coldly. You know that I have to think that you are being friendly with me again for only one reason."

She eased his arm from around her and took several brisk steps away from him.

Not to be put off, he fell into step beside her. "That's not it at all," he countered, again slipping his arm around her waist.

"I guess it would be more convincing if you would apologize for your callous behavior," Faye said icily, giving him a sideways glance.

Joe's eyes lowered. He had not wanted to apologize, fearing that apologies would lead to confessions about Kathryn. But he was damned sorry for having caused Faye such moments of embarrassment, and he did want to learn to trust her.

Slowly moving his eyes back to Faye, he knew that he must try his damnedest to make things right.

"I'm sorry, Faye," he said in a rush of words. "I never meant to hurt you. I guess it's the man in me. Men are guided by many strange sorts of feelings."

He stepped in front of her and stopped her by grabbing her by the shoulders. "Apology accepted?"

Swallowing hard, searching his handsome face, Faye was torn with emotion. She would never know why he had chosen to leave her so abruptly, and suddenly she did not care. Something told her that nothing else would stand in their way of total loving.

"*Oui*, accepted," she murmured, placing a hand gently to his cheek.

"Now I'm not saying that you can't expect me not to take you in my arms and give you a fierce loving," Joe said, his eyes twinkling. "Just when I do, remember that it is because I do love you."

Beaming, Faye smiled up at him. "I think I know that now," she said, happiness bubbling inside her. "Now, kind sir, will you please teach me how to square dance? It looks like grand fun!"

"It would be my pleasure, ma'am," Joe said, guiding her back to the gaiety of the evening.

Faye's petticoat rustled beneath her dress as Joe swept her into the circle of dancers. Her face was hot with excitement, and her eyes gleamed as she let Joe lead her into the various dance steps. She held her head back, laughing, as in her clumsiness she stepped on Joe's toes more than once while learning how to do-si-do.

When she had to change partners and leave Joe to swing someone else, Faye gave him a look of longing, and then once more was in heaven when partners were again exchanged and she found herself back with his arms around her.

Breathless, she was glad when Joe swept her away from the others. She gladly accepted a tin cup of water and gulped it down. Laughing beneath her breath, she watched Joe quickly empty his own cup, and her insides were warm as he looked at her with desire over the rim.

She scarcely breathed when Joe tossed his cup to the ground and did the same with hers. Her breath quickened with yearning as, without any words exchanged between them, Joe walked her into the shadows of the forest. Holding her at arm's length, he looked down at her. She eased her hands from his and drifted toward him, twining her arms around his neck.

"Kiss me?" she whispered. "Oh, Joe, please kiss me."

He reverently breathed her name as he lowered his mouth to her lips, then kissed her heatedly. Caught up in passion, forgetting all of the moments that she had doubted him, Faye leaned her body into his. Even through the layers of her dress and petticoat, she could feel his risen manhood strong and powerful pressed against her.

A growing heat began to tingle throughout her body. Her heart was leading her into another intimate moment with the man she loved, and she could not deny her feverish needs. There was only now. There was only Joe!

When his hands went to her buttocks and drew her harder to him, the intimate contact was almost too much for Faye to bear! A maddening passion flamed inside her.

Unable to wait a moment longer, he swung her up into his arms and began carrying her toward her wagon. She clung to his neck and pressed her cheek against his buckskin shirt, breathing in his wonderful scent. Once again the wagon would become a love nest.

But tonight would be the last time for her and Joe. Gayland would return tomorrow. She would love Joe enough tonight to last forever.

Lifting her up into the wagon, Joe climbed in after her. The light of the campfire through the canvas gave them enough light to guide them into each other's arms. With exquisite tenderness, Joe's lips drugged Faye while his hands deftly began removing her clothes. One by one the articles fell in a heap at her ankles, and he eased her down on a thick pallet of blankets.

"You're so damned beautiful," Joe whispered huskily, moving his mouth over her flesh in soft, feathery kisses. "Every inch of you is so damned beautiful."

Faye's breath was taken away when his tongue flicked over a nipple and his fingers ran down her body, causing her to sink more and more deeply into a chasm of desire. She closed her eyes and sighed as his lips moved lower with tormenting, sweet kisses. When he reached the soft tendrils of hair between her legs, Faye trembled with uncontrollable passion.

But this wondrous pleasure ended when Joe moved away from her and drew his buckskin shirt over his head. As her eyes opened, she found him looking down at her with a passion-heated gaze that sent goose pimples from her toes clean to her head.

He tossed his shirt aside and reached to remove his trousers. She enjoyed this moment of observing him in private, thrilling to the way his wide shoulders tapered to his narrow hips. Her eyes lowered then, and her breath caught in her throat when she saw the part of him that had taught her the mysteries of loving a man. His manhood was large as he knelt over her. When its velvety smoothness brushed against her thigh, an involuntary shiver, followed by a rush of pleasure, coursed through her.

"Faye, darling," Joe whispered, positioning himself over her. His hands wove through her silken hair as he drew her lips to his. "I do love you. Never doubt my love. Let me show you just how much. You, in turn, show me."

"Let's not talk of doubts of one another," Faye murmured, her pulse racing as she felt his manhood now softly probing between her thighs. "I have recently learned to detest that word. Love me, Joe. Every breath I take is yours. Please . . . love . . . me.''

A soft cry of passion escaped from between Faye's parted lips as he plunged his hardness inside her. As his dark, stormy eyes gazed down at her, she placed a hand to his cheek and smiled up at him as he began his easy strokes within her. Her breathing grew ragged when his hands cupped her breasts and his thumbs circled her nipples, drawing them into tautness.

Faye laced her arms around his neck and urged his lips to hers. Passion erupted between them as they kissed, their tongues meeting as their lips parted. With an instinct for pleasure, Faye's hips moved in unison with Joe's eager thrusts.

Raking her fingernails down his back, she moved her hands to his buttocks and splayed her fingers across his hard body. She urged him closer to her, reveling in the feel of his wondrous thrusts inside her.

And then he slowed his body and withdrew his hardness, breathing heavily as he pressed his lips to the delicate column of her throat. "I don't want it to end too soon," he whispered huskily, his tongue hot and insistent against her neck.

Ignoring his quiet command, Faye nipped at one of his nipples.

"Woman, you're driving me insane," Joe groaned, quivering with passion.

Faye moved away from his embrace and urged him to his back. Playfully, she continued to nip and lash her tongue over his straining chest. Only he was not to be teased for long. Firmly, he twined his fingers through her hair and gently urged her head downward.

Her long hair cascaded over his abdomen as he pressed her mouth to his pulsating shaft. A tremor went through her as his body stiffened and he moaned with intense pleasure.

Then his hands were at her shoulders, pulling her over him. Positioning her atop him, he filled his hands with her breasts and filled her with his hardness, thrusting into her soft, sweet core.

Faye closed her eyes and leaned her head back, receiving him with abandon as he transported her into another world where only lovers go. Fires blazed within her. His hot shaft spread warmth over her belly, over her breasts...

His strong hands on her waist, Joe guided her beneath him, and he came to her again, filling her with his hardness and moving rhythmically within her. Moving ever closer, she wrapped her legs about him, drawing him closer and more deeply inside her.

Her hands clung to his sinewed shoulders as again she found herself lost in the sensual pleasure of the moment. His lips were hot and hungry on her mouth as he kissed her wildly. His fingers dug into the flesh of her buttocks. One kiss blended into another until their bodies turned to liquid and fused into one as the explosion of release spread through them.

Clinging, Faye could hardly bear having to relinquish this moment with him. Too soon it was over.

"Please stay the night with me," she whispered, reveling in the touch of his muscled body against hers. "I want to sleep in your arms. Surely that would be heavenly." She snuggled closer. "Oh, Joe, I do love you so."

Joe kissed the hollow of her throat, then bent to kiss her breast. "But, darling, there is no storm tonight," he teased. "Surely you wouldn't be too frightened to stay by yourself."

"Fear has nothing to do with it," Faye said, sucking in her breath when his teeth gently nipped at her straining breast. "I want you here just because I want you. Nothing more."

"Does that mean that we can spend the night making love?" Joe whispered, his tongue leaving a trail of ecstasy in its wake as it moved over her trembling flesh. "Or have you had enough?"

"Never will I ever have enough of you," Faye murmured, closing her eyes as his lips now worshiped her body. "Joe Harrison, you could quickly spoil me, you know."

"Exactly," he teased, his hands cupping and kneading her breasts as his lips moved lower across her abdomen. "Just you watch me."

Faye sighed deeply and let him have his way with her, happiness spreading from deep within her. She closed her eyes and greedily enjoyed the singing and soaring of her flesh. When she felt him enter her again, thrusting deeply, she yielded herself to him, lost in the savagery of his kiss as he gathered her in his arms.

Fiercely, he held her close, and this time the pleasure came much more quickly, leaving them both weak and satiated.

Joe drew her to his side as they came down from their cloud of bliss. "Darling, it shouldn't take many more days to reach Fort Smith," he said softly, his fingers toying with soft curls at her temple. "What then? What are your plans?"

Faye turned and snuggled against him, sighing. "Only that I hope they include you," she murmured. "They will, won't they, Joe?"

"I'd shoot anyone who might try to get in my way," Joe threatened throatily. "But of course there's no problem with that, is there, Faye?"

He leaned closer, looking into her eyes. "Do you realize I've never even asked about this brother of yours? What did you say his name was?"

Faye looked adoringly up at him. She traced his lips with her finger. "Surely you know him. His name is Michael Poincaré. He's the one who established a mission in the area way before Fort Smith was there."

Faye winced as Joe jerked up away from her and scowled down at her, his fingers nervously raking through his hair. "Father Michael is your brother?" he asked, his voice drawn. "Yes, why didn't I make the connection? When you told me your last name, I should have known. You see, to most your brother goes by the name of Father Michael. Hardly anyone ever even recalls his last name."

He stared down at her, speechless. There had been enough strain between him and Faye without him voicing aloud his feelings for the priest who did much more than preach the gospel.

No. He would wait until they reached Fort Smith to let her know his true feelings for her brother. But he must tell her then. Her life could be threatened by the dangerous habits of Father Michael.

Faye moved to sit beside Joe, studying him. Something turned cold inside her. Surely Michael was admired by everyone. For a decade the mission had been the only place people could seek aid in time of trouble before the fort had been established.

"Joe, what aren't you saying?" she asked, her spine stiffening when she saw that his expression had not softened.

He gave her a pensive stare. Then, not wanting anything to stand between them, especially now, Joe drew Faye back into his arms. "Darling, you're imagining things," he crooned. "Now let's not talk anymore about brothers. Don't we have better things to do?''

Faye snuggled. ''What do you have in mind?'' she whispered, trembling as his hand cupped her breast.

''This,'' Joe said, lowering her back down to the pallet of blankets.

Chapter Eleven

Fort Smith, Arkansas

A handful of log cabins were scattered across the land as the wagon train drew closer to Fort Smith. In the distance the Arkansas River twisted and turned, the bluffs towering majestically above it.

Faye was torn with emotion as she sat on the wagon seat beside Celia. Anxiety spread through every nerve. Troubling thoughts of how she would cope with life in the wilderness were close to spoiling the reunion between brother and sister.

She glanced over at Celia as she clung to Gayland's arm, so proud that he was well and strong again. They were the lucky ones. They were arriving to the vast wilderness as a couple.

Stifling a sob, Faye jerked her eyes away from the contented couple, wondering what the future held for her and Joe. There had been many stolen moments these past weeks, but no commitment. Joe had backed off from talking of marriage. Just when she had begun to fully trust him Joe had withdrawn.

Her eyes widened at the sight of a small log and stone stockade situated on a rocky bluff overlooking the junction of the Poteau and Arkansas Rivers. A cluster of huts and houses had grown up around it. Fort Smith had been finally reached!

"We're there!" Celia cried excitedly. "I can't believe it. The journey is over."

Faye's gaze went to Joe, who rode ahead, directing the caravan of wagons across a bridge and into the courtyard. As Gayland's wagon took its turn in line to travel over the bridge, Faye looked over the town. Dismay lit her eyes. At best it was rustic and undesirable.

A wide street split the town in two. Low stone and wooden buildings, among which saloons were noticeably abundant, lined each side. Boardwalks on each side of the dirt street were lined with hitching posts, horses reined to them. Faye could hear the faint sound of voices coming from the saloons, along with the jangling of pianos and shrill laughs of women.

Her attention was drawn to several men as they began to gather at the doorways of the saloons and stores to gape at the arrival of the wagon train. Then women dressed in all sorts of bright garb, their faces painted, rushed from the bordellos to flirt and tease the soldiers, some of the women going so far as to pull themselves atop the horses.

After hungry kisses were shamefully exchanged, the soldiers tossed the women to the ground and rode on across the bridge and into the fort. Faye felt a sudden sickness invade her. This was Joe's world.

Her thoughts were quickly diverted by the clatter of wagon wheels on the wooden bridge. Soon they would be entering the courtyard. Was her brother Michael there, waiting? Would he be happy to see her, or would she just be an interference in his life?

Faye looked anxiously around her, studying faces, but not yet seeing Michael. Several buildings had been constructed inside the fort walls, one of which was most prominent.

She read the sign above the door. "Nicks and Rogers," she whispered, realizing this was a post store Joe had talked about. It had been established by Thomas Rogers, an ex-army captain, and Colonel John Nicks.

The store carried on a profitable trade with the Indians and settlers. In it one could find supplies for the house and garden and abundant food. As a gathering place, the post store had quickly become a source for news, not only for goings-on in the territory but also news from down river and back East.

Shifting her gaze, Faye saw the magazine, the storehouse for military supplies. Constructed of stone, its walls were more than a foot thick.

"Faye? Faye Poincaré?"

Faye's eyes snapped back around as Gayland drew the wagon to a halt. She had not noticed a man attired in a black robe with a stiffly starched white collar step from the post store and cross the courtyard to stop beside her. Faye's insides grew warm when she looked down at her brother.

Speechless, Faye covered her mouth with a hand and sucked in a nervous breath as her gaze searched his face, seeing his familiar hawklike nose, deep-set blue eyes and receding hair that had turned prematurely gray by age thirty-five.

"Well?" Michael said, his eyes twinkling as he held his arms out to her. "Aren't you glad to see me, sister?"

"Oh, Michael, it is really you," Faye finally said, hurriedly climbing from the wagon. She lunged into her brother's arms and clung to him. "It's been so long," she sobbed, pressing her cheek hard against his chest. "I'm so glad to see you. *Comment vas-tu?* Why did you stay away from the family for so long?"

"Faye, you know that I have my duties," he said hoarsely, holding her at arm's length. His gaze swept over her appraisingly, as though he was seeing her for the very first time. He admired her long, dark hair that was parted and pulled back from her face, falling in curls to her shoulders, her brilliant blue eyes, her pale yellow calico dress.

"You've grown up into a woman since I last saw you," he said. "Now I see that my responsibilities to you will be twofold. There are a lot of dangerous men in these parts. I must make sure not a one gets his hands on you."

Past his shoulder, Faye caught sight of Joe. He glared at her, then turned angrily on his heel and swung himself up into his saddle and rode from the courtyard and through the wide gate with Bart Dobbs riding alongside him.

"Faye? What's the matter?" Michael asked. He glanced over his shoulder, seeing nothing that drew his attention, then looked questioningly back at Faye as she smiled awkwardly up at him. "What did you see? Is there something wrong?"

She was reprieved from the strain of the moment when Celia bounced from the wagon and came to her side, her green eyes vivacious and her auburn hair drawn back with a green bow that matched her cotton dress.

"Faye, this has to be your brother. Will you please introduce us?" Celia flashed Michael a warm, sweet smile. "Sir, I must say my husband and I have become quite attached to your sister. If not for her, I doubt if I could have stood the horrible ordeal. She's been a blessing."

Taking Celia's hand and clasping it fondly, Faye made the proper introductions, then when Gayland stepped up beside her, did the same with him. "Michael, I would like to ask a special favor of you," she said softly, imploring him with her eyes. "Instead of my friends having to live in their wagon while a house is being constructed, would you possibly have room at the rectory for them? It would be so kind if you would let them stay in more comfortable quarters."

Michael slipped an arm around Faye's waist and drew her to his side. "I see no problem with that suggestion," he said softly. "Then we'll see that a house raising begins soon. That always gives everyone cause for socializing in these parts."

Faye warmed at his words and moved closer to him, reveling in his nearness.

"That's so kind of you, sir," Celia said, clasping her hands anxiously together behind her.

Gayland reached out to shake the priest's hand. "Your kindness will be rewarded, Father," he said thickly. "I'll do whatever I can to help around the rectory and church. Just ask. I'm your man. I'm good with my hands."

"I appreciate that," Michael said, then swung Faye away from him and eyed his horse and buggy. "You just follow me in your wagon, and Faye and I will direct you to the mission. It's only a short distance from the fort."

Lifting the hem of her dress, Faye walked to the horse and buggy. She forced a smile as Michael helped her up onto the buggy seat. Sitting with her back straight, she flipped her hair away from her shoulders and tried to be happy now that she was with her brother again. The dreaded trip was behind her. She would be bathing in a tub and sleeping in a bed tonight. Surely she should be happy.

But she wasn't. Thoughts of Joe plagued her with her every heartbeat....

A great stone wall enclosed the church and rectory. Faye walked with Michael from the buggy toward the rectory, a large two-story house of limestone built around a courtyard. The roof was constructed of neatly sawed shingles, and a chimney jutted at one end. An outside stairway on the other side of the house led to a large attic where any travelers who were passing by were welcome to stay in cold or wet weather.

Faye looked over at the church—a great wooden structure that stood proudly separate from the rectory. A tower and elaborate stone statues decorated the exterior.

Farther back from the two main buildings stood a row of low, squat wooden cabins and a stable.

Everywhere Faye looked people were busy with some sort of activity, from brushing down horses to hanging laundry on a line close to the rectory. She smiled at a Mexican boy as he rushed up to Michael, his eyes wide with excitement. Michael patted him fondly on the head and instructed him to help Gayland unload the wagon and take Faye's personal belongings into his study.

Faye walked on into the rectory with Michael, awed by its loveliness. It had all the comforts of New Orleans, and Faye was suddenly swept up into feelings of having just arrived home.

As they stepped into the study, Faye admired the rich tapestry that hung on the wall between the windows, and then moved her gaze on around the room where plush furniture sat in front of a blazing fire in the fireplace. The floors were covered with thick Indian rugs, and there was an aroma of fresh flowers in the room, drawing Faye's eyes to a massive arrangement of roses and lilacs in a vase on Michael's large oak desk.

"You seem pleased enough," Michael said, going to a cabinet and removing two long-stemmed glasses. Pouring wine into each, he took one to Faye. "Now it's not going to be all that hard to adjust to living with your brother, is it?"

Faye laughed nervously, accepting the glass. "I must say I did not expect anything like this," she said, sipping the wine. "I would have thought that you might be poor, Michael. But it seems that I was wrong."

"God and his people have been good to me," Michael said, nodding to the young Mexican lad as boxes of Faye's belongings were carried into the room and deposited on the rug. "Except that He saw fit to take our parents from us. Who can ever understand why anyone as gentle and caring as our mother and father had to die? The world is full of so many who do not deserve to live.''

A shiver coursed through Faye as she found it hard to believe that he would talk of anyone's death so coldly, even an outlaw's. But then she reminded herself of just how many sadnesses he must have experienced out here in the wilderness. Could that cause even a priest to become less feeling?

''Michael, I never want to see a paddlewheel boat again!'' she exclaimed bitterly, thinking back to their parents' untimely death. ''When word was received of the explosion of the *Delta*, I couldn't believe it. Mother and Father so loved to travel on the Mississippi. You know how Father loved to dabble in gambling, and there was a lot of gambling on the *Delta*.''

''Yes, I know,'' Michael growled, pouring himself another glass of wine. ''I argued with him about that weakness, but he never listened. It seems that his love of gambling paid off, but not in the way he had expected.''

Faye's eyes pooled with tears. ''Please, Michael,'' she murmured, ''don't talk like that. Let's not even speak of the *Delta* again, or any boats like it. Out here in this wilderness I'm far away from all remembrances of the accident.''

Michael eyed her quietly. It was apparent that she hadn't heard about the arrival of the first steamboat to Fort Smith in April. But of course she wouldn't have. She had been in transit from New Orleans to Fort Smith when the steamboat had arrived. The river steamer had been the *Robert Thompson*. It had arrived towing a keelboat loaded with commissary supplies and carrying an officer of the army paymaster corps with the garrison payroll.

The *Robert Thompson* had cast off from Pittsburgh on St. Patrick's Day and reached Little Rock on April 9 and Fort Smith on April 20. Navigation of the Arkansas River by steamboat all the way to Fort Smith would mean much faster communication with the East and would also assure faster delivery of mail, supplies and would bring more settlers to the area.

"Yes, let's not speak any more of that tragic river accident," Michael said, placing his glass on a table beside him. He spied the few boxes that sat at Faye's feet, and then her trunk. "Were you able to bring as many of your personal belongings as you wanted? You did not have much space in the wagon for yourself, did you, honey?"

Faye bent to her knees and unclasped her trunk and slowly opened its lid. "I auctioned off most that was dear to us, Michael," she said, her voice breaking. "I had no other choice. But I did bring you a couple of mementoes."

Her fingers trembling, she searched beneath her silk finery and found two small boxes. Moving to her feet, she handed one of the boxes to Michael and held on to the other one. "Open this one first," she said dryly. "It's something precious, Michael. It was a gift from you to Mother many, many years ago."

She watched eagerly as Michael opened the box and his eyes misted with tears. He withdrew a handkerchief trimmed with delicate lace and embroidered with their mother's initials. The aroma of their mother's perfume still clung to the linen.

Michael drew the handkerchief up to his nose and inhaled the fragrance, closing his eyes, envisioning his mother.

Then he blinked and laid the handkerchief aside to take the other box that Faye offered him. His fingers were coldly numb as he opened this box and looked down at a well-used pocket knife. Quickly he looked up at Faye.

"It's the one I gave Father that day long ago when we were fishing," he said hoarsely. "It had been a gift to me from a friend, but when I saw that Father didn't have a knife to cut his own line, I gave him my knife and told him to keep it. I'll never forget the look in his eyes. He had known the importance of that knife to me. Donald, my very best friend in the world at that time, had given it to me and had just recently died. Father cherished that knife. I'm glad it wasn't on him when he died. It means a lot to me to have it again.''

Faye lowered her eyes and gulped back a tear. "Oh, but it was," she murmured. "It was one of the items recovered when his body was found."

Michael placed the knife aside and drew Faye into his arms. He held her close. "Sister, things will be all right," he said softly. "We're together. For now you'll need nobody else. I'll make life for you quite grand here at the mission. There are so many things to do that you won't have time to ponder over Mother and Father's deaths again."

He looked at her intently. "But I don't know how you'll ever find a fine enough young man for you in these parts," he said, his voice drawn. "The soldiers are wild, chasing those senseless women in the bordellos as if there was no tomorrow."

He didn't want to say that the bordellos were not the only attractions that drew the soldiers. There were also the crude saloons where the trappers, hunters and farmers could always find a large supply of homemade whiskey. The army troops spent nearly all their free time gambling and drinking, and in most cases ended up drunk in the fort's guardhouse.

Michael blamed these unruly times on the army and its interference in the area. The mission had offered a peaceful outlet for the men in the community before the fort had arrived.

"I can't think of anyone else at this moment that I would even allow to come calling on you," he said, getting back to the main point of the conversation. "But let's not worry about nonsense like that. You're here safe and sound. That's all that matters."

Michael poured himself another glass of wine, guided Faye into a chair and sat down beside her. "And for God's sake, Faye, don't ever get around those two scouts who work for the army," he said, frowning. "I'm sure you know who I am speaking of. Didn't Joe Harrison and Bart Dobbs help escort the wagon train from the Mississippi border?"

Faye paled, inhaling a shaky breath as she avoided his eyes. "Yes, they were the scouts," she said dryly, then looked him square in the eye. "Why do you find them so intolerable, Michael?"

She scarcely breathed as she awaited his reply, but to her surprise there was none. He turned his gaze to the fireplace and stared into the dancing flames.

Her heart pounding, she also stared into the fire but all she saw were Joe's wonderfully dark, passion-glazed eyes.

Joe paced in his cabin, trying to shake the memory of Faye embracing Father Michael. Seeing them together made him aware of just how hard it was to accept that Father Michael was her brother. Because of Joe's bitter differences with Father Michael, the relationship between him and Faye was going to be strained. Father Michael might even forbid him from seeing her. It had been enough for Joe to have to worry about Faye's not being able to adjust to the wilderness way of life, now he also had to worry about how Father Michael would turn Faye against him.

Eyeing a trunk at the far side of the room, Joe sauntered toward it then braced himself on one knee and opened it. Removing a lacy wedding dress, he fingered it, hurt burning his loins. It hadn't been enough that Kathryn had left him just prior to the wedding, but then her father had seen fit to bring her dress to him.

With a sigh of despair, he threw the dress down and grabbed a bottle.

Pouring himself a shot of whiskey, he slouched down into a chair before the fire and began to drink with abandon. He fervently hoped that before the night was through, he would be too damned drunk to think about anything, least of all Faye Poincaré.

Chapter Twelve

The sky was overcast with low-hanging gray clouds. The wind was crisp and cool for the month of June. A fringed shawl pulled snugly around her shoulders and her fingers clutching the crude seat of the buckboard wagon, Faye entered the wide gate of the fort, glad that Michael had included her in his outing to get supplies for the mission. Perhaps this would give her an opportunity to catch a glimpse of Joe. It had now been a week since their arrival, and she had not heard one word from him.

In her dress of blue organdy and her bonnet tied neatly under her chin with a blue ribbon, Faye became aware of the solders' attentions. She looked down to see the appreciation in the eyes of the soldiers who had paused from their duties to stare openly at her.

Blushing, Faye was glad when the post store was reached so that she could escape inside it. Michael drew rein in front of the boardwalk and sidled his buckboard wagon up to the hitching rail. After climbing down and draping his horse's reins around the rail, he went to Faye and offered her his hand to assist her from the wagon.

"I guess I can understand why you insisted on coming with me today," he said, glancing around uneasily. "You are surely missing your shopping sprees in New Orleans."

"*Oui*," Faye said, trying not to reveal that this was not at all the reason that she had come with him. Joe was the reason. Only Joe. If she didn't see him soon, she would be forced to go and find him. With a few sly questions, she had discovered where he made his residence. It was not at all far from the mission.

"Well, sister, I'm afraid you're going to be disappointed," Michael said, slipping an arm possessively around her waist and walking her toward the door. "You won't find an assortment of dresses to your liking here at Nicks and Rogers. They mainly carry bolts of material for the women to sew their own dresses." He gave Faye an amused smile. "How many dresses have you made in your lifetime?" he teased.

"Michael, that's not fair," Faye said, her eyes dancing. "You know there was no need in my learning. Embroidery is the only sewing needle that Mother introduced me to."

"Yes, I am aware of that," Michael said dryly. "I always felt that was a mistake. Those of us who were raised in a home filled with riches usually have the hardest time adjusting.''

Faye gave him a troubled glance. ''But, Michael, you left home and are quite successful in your new environment,'' she murmured. ''I hope I will be, too, in time. Don't you think that's possible?''

''You made the long and arduous journey from New Orleans in the face of many dangers and came through it unscathed,'' Michael said, smiling down at her. ''I believe you have proved that you and I are of the same blood. Though Mother and Father did spoil you, they instilled the better traits in you, also. You were born with courage and willpower and a drive to succeed.'' He nodded. ''*Oui*, you will persevere.''

''I hope you are right,'' Faye said, smiling a thank-you to Michael as he opened the door for her. ''At times I miss New Orleans so badly that I ache inside. Though you did not approve of the fancy balls, I so adored dressing up in gowns and attending them.''

''I have changed my view on dancing somewhat,'' Michael declared. ''Out here in the wilderness there are hardly any chances for socializing. When there is a reason for everyone to gather together, I wholeheartedly approve of them dancing. It does my heart good to see everyone have a good time.''

His eyes twinkled as he looked down at her. ''But even though there are occasional dances, no fancy dresses are required here. Perhaps you will be content enough today in just choosing a new bonnet?''

Lifting the hem of her dress, Faye walked beneath the antlers that hung over the doorway and moved across the threshold into the store. She was quickly amazed at how well the store was stocked. In one quick glance Faye saw crockery and cookware, bolts of colorful material, dried fruits, coffee, leather, molasses, rope and fresh-cut plug tobacco. Her eyes leaped from patent medicines to plow handles, from guitar strings to chimneys for kerosene lamps.

Then she turned and looked around her. The room was narrow and dim. She squinted, but could not make out who was standing in the darkest shadows, sorting through the equipment.

Her gaze went to several customers who lingered around a potbellied wood stove. Dressed in dark breeches and cotton shirts, they were obviously settlers. Some were smoking pipes, others were sipping coffee. And since the room was devoid of women besides Faye, she again became the focal point of attention.

Nervously shifting her eyes away from the men, Faye's fullest attention was drawn to a glass showcase where beaded hatpins and jet belt buckles lured her with their glitter beneath the glow of the kerosene lamps.

Going to the case, Faye leaned closer and viewed the assortment of laces and ribbons.

"I think you've got enough to look at to occupy you while I go to the blacksmith shop," Michael said, patting Faye affectionately on the hand. "Do you mind? My business with the blacksmith won't take long, and I'd rather not include you in it."

He smiled over at John Rogers and nodded a silent hello. "John will see to your needs as soon as he finishes his transaction with another customer," he reassured. He bent to kiss Faye's cheek. "Honey, choose whatever you like. I'll buy it for you as a welcoming gift."

Faye turned to Michael. Her eyes misted with tears, for his gentleness reminded her so much of their father. Moving into his embrace, she hugged him fondly. "No gift is needed," she murmured. "Michael, that I am here safe with you is enough. I missed you, Michael. Let's never be separated by miles again."

Michael returned her hug, then eased her from his arms. "Nothing will separate us again," he said, looking solemnly down at her. "Nothing."

Wiping a stray tear from her eye, Faye watched him walk away from her, his black robe swishing at his ankles.

Then, turning her eyes back to the case of women's accessories, Faye began to look the sun bonnets over very carefully. The lace was crisp and gathered on one she especially liked, the velveteen smooth and soft on another.

Undraping her shawl from around her shoulders and placing it on the counter, she then removed her own bonnet and laid it with her shawl. Standing in front of the mirror next to the display, she placed first one bonnet and then another on her head, observing each very carefully in the mirror. Deciding on the one with the lace trim, she tied the bonnet's ribbons beneath her chin and tilted her head one way and then another, pleased with her reflection.

"I would say you made the right choice."

Faye's heartbeat quickened when she recognized the voice and then saw Joe's reflection in the mirror beside hers.

"Joe!" Faye murmured, turning to face him.

Joe's large hands moved to the bonnet, rearranging it just slightly and smoothing some curls from beneath it so that they lay in tight ringlets at her brow. "Now that's even lovelier," he said, smiling down at her.

"Joe, how long have you been watching?" Faye asked, her face warming with a blush.

"Not long," Joe said, lifting a muscled shoulder in a casual shrug. "How long have you been here?"

"Not long," Faye said, laughing lightly.

"Did you come to the post store to purchase yourself a new bonnet?" he asked, fishing inside his front pocket for coins. "Let me do you the honor. Let me buy it for you."

Still puzzled by his recent absence, Faye untied the ribbon beneath her chin and eased the bonnet from her head.

"No, thank you," she said somberly. "I have decided against this bonnet or any of these others that I have been trying on."

Again, Joe shrugged. The coins clinked as he dropped them back into his pocket. "And how are things at the mission?" he asked, a cold edge to his voice. "Are you settled in?"

Faye fitted her own bonnet back onto her head, hating the fact that her fingers trembled as she tied the bow. "Do you truly care if I am or am not settled in?" she finally said, turning her back to him to gaze into the mirror as she primped. "You have shown no interest in anything that I've done since my arrival to this ghastly place." She turned slowly around and gave him a set stare. "What would you say if I asked you what has been taking up your time, both day *and* night?"

Joe returned her challenging stare for a moment, then raked his eyes over her, taking in her supple figure. He had purposely stayed away from her because he had wanted her to have time to adjust to this new life. Too, he had dreaded going to the mission to ask to see her, all along knowing what Father Michael's reaction would be.

"I was taken away again for a few days," Joe lied, nervously raking his fingers through his thick, dark hair. "Business. I'm sorry if I troubled you. But I'm back and would like tǒ see you, Faye. Perhaps even tonight?"

Faye's heart thumped wildly, and she smiled up at him. "*Oui*, Joe, tonight would be lovely," she said in a soft purr, then her smile faded. "But, Joe, where is there to go for a night out? All that I saw in town were saloons and brothels."

Joe frowned down at her, knowing that in her mind's eye she was comparing the town of Fort Smith to New Orleans, and anyone would know which one would most definitely come up short.

"Faye, since there are no fancy ballrooms to escort you to, I guess you may just have to lower yourself to spend an evening in my cabin, sitting by the fire and chatting," he said hoarsely. "Now I guess I could strum the guitar for you for entertainment." He leaned down closer to her and smiled seductively. "But, of course, I had better things on my mind."

Faye had at first been rankled by his mocking reference to ballrooms, but his final hint of what he truly had planned for the evening caused her cheeks to burn with embarrassment. Shifting her feet nervously, Faye eyed the door, thinking it best to continue this discussion elsewhere. "Joe, let's get a breath of fresh air," she suggested softly, hurrying toward the entrance.

Just outside the door they both stopped short at the sight of Michael making his way toward them from the blacksmith shop. His eyes were two points of fire as he glared from Faye to Joe.

"Perhaps it's best not to discuss this evening right now," Faye said.

"I don't believe in putting off matters that are of prime importance," Joe said, grabbing her by the shoulders and turning her so that their eyes met and held. "Will you come with me tonight or won't you?"

"Unhand her this minute," Michael growled, stepping up on the boardwalk beside Faye and placing an arm possessively around her waist. "Joe Harrison, my sister has been warned against the likes of you. Now you've been warned, also."

Joe's stomach coiled tightly. He curled his hands into tight fists at his sides. "Father Michael, you..." he began, but was stopped when a shrill whistle tore through the air from the direction of the river.

At the sound of the riverboat whistle, Faye's knees grew weak, and her vision blurred with sudden tears. It was the same whistle that the *Delta* had sounded over and over again, warning the city of the catastrophe.

She gave Michael a pleading, questioning glance. "Michael, the whistle," she cried softly. "It's a riverboat. I didn't know riverboats came to these parts.''

''I didn't tell you,'' Michael said in a low apology. ''I had hoped by the time the boat returned you would have had time to get over your terror.''

The blast of the whistle sent goose pimples across Faye's flesh. She placed her hands over her ears. ''No!'' she whispered, trying to shake the horrible memory. ''No!''

Wildly she began to run toward Michael's buckboard wagon. ''Michael, take me home!'' she cried. ''Oh, please take me home!''

Michael gave Joe a troubled glance, then rushed to the wagon, grabbed his reins and hurriedly drove the wagon away from the fort.

Joe watched, stunned. He had not realized that her pain ran so deep. She had spoken of how she missed her parents, but never had she displayed such torment.

He kneaded his brow, jealous that Michael was the one she sought for comfort.

Lumbering toward his reined horse, Joe was stopped when John Rogers came rushing from his store. Joe eyed the shawl Rogers held in his hand, recognizing it as Faye's.

''Joe, the lady you were talking with left her shawl behind,'' he said, holding it out to Joe. ''Would you mind returning it to her? I'm afraid if I left it here to give it to her later, it might get lost in the shuffle or get sold to someone by mistake.''

Joe took the shawl, its softness in his calloused hand reminding him of Faye. "I'll see that she gets it," he said, his voice drawn. "Thanks, John. She'll appreciate it."

John, a short, balding man, toyed with his mustache as his dark eyes gleamed. "Mighty pretty thing," he commented, smiling. "Is she some relation to Father Michael?"

Once again fire entered Joe's eyes. His fingers tightened about the shawl. "You have it figured right," he growled. "Father Michael's her brother."

"Reckon she's single?" John further questioned.

"Not for long," Joe said, setting his jaw firmly. "Not if I have anything to say about it."

He turned on his heel and strode toward his horse. "And Michael will fight me all the way to the altar," he growled under his breath, swinging himself up into his saddle.

Chapter Thirteen

Firelight flickered over the furniture from a stone fireplace in the corner of the bedroom. Faye stood with her back to the flames, her gaze moving to the French doors that led out to the terrace. Though it was night and the air was chilly, she longed to step outside and gaze up at the moon. Somewhere not far away in the forest, the same moon shone over Joe's cabin.

Looking for her shawl, Faye was suddenly aware that she had not brought it with her from the fort. When she had left the post store, she had left the shawl lying on the counter.

Disgruntled at herself for losing yet another shawl, she grabbed her cape and moved out to the terrace. She looked up at the sky and felt a keen loneliness sweep through her. Choking back a sob, she let herself get lost in the memories of her nights with Joe and of how he had filled her with pleasure with each kiss, with each embrace, and with the ultimate union of their shared passion. . . .

Standing before the fireplace in his cabin, Joe clasped his fingers around Faye's shawl, trying to devise a plan to return it to her. If he went to the mission, he would have to ask Father Michael's permission to see Faye, and he did not take kindly to having to ask that hypocrite for permission to do anything. His blood boiled when he even thought of having to come face-to-face with Father Michael again.

He slung the shawl over the back of a chair and bent to his knee before the fireplace. One by one he began to lay fresh logs atop the burning coals.

A commotion outside drew Joe quickly to his feet. He placed his hands on his hips and glowered at Bart as he staggered into the cabin with two feisty, voluptuous saloon girls clinging to each arm.

Cheap perfume wafted across the room as Joe's gaze burned along the flesh of the women who giggled and eyed him seductively. Scarcely clothed, they wore only their bright dance hall garments that were cut so low that all but the nipples of their breasts were exposed to the eye.

Their faces were gaudy with rouge and lipstick, and black lace stockings clung to their shapely legs where the hems of their gathered dresses lay way above their knees. Inexpensive ear clips and necklaces sparkled in the dim light of the kerosene lamp hanging from the ceiling, its wick turned low.

Bart shook himself free of the women and stumbled drunkenly over to Joe. Laughing throatily, he patted Joe on the shoulder and leaned close as he spoke into his face. "I got us two of the best for tonight," he drawled. He hiccuped, then laughed at himself for it, leaning closer to Joe. "One's for you, and one's for me. Which one do you want, Joe? Take your pick." He chuckled and gave the girls a quick look over his shoulder. "Now ain't I generous, ladies? I'm givin' my best friend the pick of the litter tonight."

Joe placed his hands on Bart's shoulders and pushed him away. "I'm not in the mood for this, Bart," he growled, turning his eyes from their saucy expressions.

"Not in the mood?" Bart said, taken aback. "Whenever has Joe Harrison not been in the mood for a woman?"

Joe frowned at Bart. "All right, let me reword that," he grumbled. "I'm in the mood, but not for these floozies. You damned well know who I'd like to be with tonight."

Bart cleared his throat and adjusted his gun belt and stepped closer to Joe, appearing to have sobered just a bit. "Joe, I know who you're speakin' of, and that's why I brought you a woman," he said blandly. "As I see it, these past few days you've needed to get Faye out of your blood." He gestured with a swing of his hand toward the women. "I can't see a better time than now. Darlene there with the red hair will make you forget everything but her skills at makin' love." He leaned into Joe's face. "I know," he whispered. "I've had her more than once myself."

Joe stepped away and found the door. Holding it open with his foot, he pushed first one then the other out into the night. "Like I said, I'm not in the mood."

Bart swayed drunkenly and seemed as though he was about to argue the point. Then thinking better of it, he grinned on one side and slapped his friend on the shoulder. "Joe, you got it bad." Then stepping outside and grabbing hold of both women, he slurred over his shoulder, "But I sure got it good!"

His face flushed with anger, Joe slammed the door shut and cast an angry gaze about the now empty cabin. His eyes shifted to the fringed shawl. He picked it up and placed it beneath his nose and sniffed the familiar sweet scent of Faye clinging to it.

"I'm going to take it to her," he whispered. "I've got to see her. Tonight!"

Riding through the open gate of the mission, Joe stopped his horse just outside the rectory and slipped out of his saddle to the ground. Tying his horse to a hitching rail, he studied the rectory in the darkness, seeing several windows golden with lamplight on both the first and second floor. Somewhere in the night someone was strumming a guitar. The mission seemed very peaceful on this June night.

Thus far the outlaws had not taken undue advantage of Father Michael's generous ways, but if Michael continued to fuel the fires of the vigilante movement, it would inevitably happen. If Father Michael did not change his ways, this mission might one day soon be without the priest they so cherished.

But that was not his concern at the moment. Tonight he had not come with warnings for Father Michael. He had come for Faye.

Joe removed Faye's shawl from his saddlebag and draped it across his arm. Boldly stepping up to the door, he raised the brass knocker and let it drop with a loud thud. He repeated this two and three more times, then stood back and waited. When the door opened, Michael stood in the foyer, looking holy in his black robe, his gray hair smoothed back from his brow. Joe tensed and glared at him.

"Joe Harrison!" Michael gasped. "What is your business?"

Joe eased past him and into the grand house. He craned his neck and looked into the parlor, then toward the staircase at the far end of the foyer before turning to face Michael. He gestured with the shawl. "Faye forgot this when she was shopping at the post store,'' he said thickly. "I've come to return it to her. I'd like to do it in person, Michael. Will you announce my presence, or must I be forced to go and find her myself?''

Michael's spine stiffened, and his eye lit with anger. "What did I tell you earlier?'' he said angrily. "You're to stay away from Faye." He then leaned closer to Joe. "Now get on out of here," he warned, hardly able to hold his temper any longer.

Joe chuckled. "You're not behaving in a very Christian manner," he taunted. "And where's that hospitality that you preach? You're being way less than hospitable to me, Father Michael.''

"As I've been given cause *not* to be," Michael growled. He reached for the shawl. "I can deliver the shawl to Faye myself. Now go on your way. I don't want the likes of you at my mission.''

"I thought the mission was open to everyone,'' Joe pressed. "That should not exclude me, now should it?''

"You, sir, are an exception," Michael said coldly. "You aren't the sort to listen to reason of any kind. And as for Faye, she's not like the whores you bed. You keep your hands off her, Joe. She's too good for you, and you know it.''

Joe's jaw tightened. "Father Michael, now you know damned well that if I don't see Faye tonight, I will later. What's it to be? Now or later?''

"It had better be never."

The sound of a horse arriving at the mission had caused Faye to move from the terrace to her room. Tossing her cape aside and slipping into a robe, she left her room and crept down the long, narrow hallway. At the head of the staircase, she froze in her steps at the sound of the cool, measured tones of her brother...and Joe Harrison.

Inching to the banister, she looked down just as Joe suddenly thrust something into Michael's arms and turned and fled from the house.

Her heartbeat anxious, Faye rushed down the stairs, crying out Joe's name. But when her brother turned and gave her a cold look, her footsteps faltered, and she felt as though a stranger were looking up at her.

Placing a hand to her throat she moved on down the stairs much more slowly. When she reached the first floor, she saw what had brought Joe to the rectory.

"My shawl!" she gasped. "I realized just a short while ago that I had left it at the post store."

Michael thrust the shawl into Faye's arms. "That's not the sole purpose for Joe Harrison coming here this time of night," he said in a low growl. "Sister, just what went on between you and that man while traveling to Fort Smith? When I was warning you against him earlier, you knew that you had already made more than a mere acquaintance with him. Do you want to tell me about it, or do I come to my own conclusions?''

Faye's face reddened with a blush. ''Michael, you can come to whatever conclusions you want about me and Joe Harrison,'' she stated flatly. ''Must I remind you that I am no longer a mere child? I know how to choose my own acquaintances. Just because you are almost twice my age does not give you the right to behave as my father.''

''Faye, you are now my responsibility,'' Michael said, his voice softer. ''I must urge you not to see that man. He's wild and no good. Surely you already know that.''

Oui, that was so, Faye admitted to herself. But she had found ways of taming him.

''Oh, Michael,'' Faye pleaded, moving to lay her face against his chest, ''I only just arrived. Please let's get along. You are all the kin I have left in the world. Make me glad. Oh, make me glad.''

Michael circled an arm around Faye's waist and held her close. ''I'm sorry for being so harsh with you,'' he apologized. ''But Joe Harrison seems to bring out the worst in me.''

''Why?'' Faye asked, leaning back, searching her brother's face.

''It's not something I like to discuss,'' Michael

said, disengaging himself from their embrace. "For tonight let's let this rest. All right?"

Faye moved toward the staircase, clutching the shawl. "*Oui*, for tonight," she murmured.

Chapter Fourteen

It was early morning, and Faye sighed with relief as she watched Michael leave on his buckboard wagon with supplies that he planned to distribute to needy settlers. She was already dressed for her journey to Joe's, hoping that she would find him home and willing to talk with her.

"Faye, what are you watching so intently from the window?"

Celia's silent approach having momentarily frightened her, Faye smiled awkwardly. Smoothing her hands down the gathers of her gingham dress, she walked toward her good friend, who had seemed so happy since their arrival at the mission. Plans were being made to have a house-raising for Celia and Gayland. It was something every new settler looked forward to—a place of their own.

Faye took Celia's hands and squeezed them fondly. "I was watching Michael," she murmured. "He just left. Are you sure you don't mind covering for me if he returns home before I do? You won't feel too uncomfortable telling Michael an untruth . . . that I am in my room, embroidering, should he inquire about me?"

"No, I don't mind that," Celia said, her smile fading. "But I can't say that I agree with what you are planning to do. Are you certain you want to take off all by yourself in this wilderness?" Her eyelashes fluttered nervously. "I've heard there are swamps that swallow horses whole if one ventures too close!"

Faye slipped her hands from Celia's and went back to the window. The open gate leading out to the forest seemed to beckon to her. Though everything Celia said was true, nothing would stop her. She had waited long enough to see Joe. He had come for her last evening. Nothing would keep them apart today.

"Celia, you would go to the ends of the earth to be with Gayland, wouldn't you?" she said, turning to face Celia. "I feel the same about Joe Harrison. I have decided to fight tooth and nail for him. This past week I've been miserable without him."

Celia paled and placed her hand to her throat. "You love him that much?" she gasped. "Though he has so little to offer you? Faye, living the life of the affluent in New Orleans, you are used to so much more than what Joe Harrison could surely ever offer you. Can you honestly say that you will be able to live with so little?"

"How can you ask that?" Faye said, frowning. "When one is in love, isn't having the man all that is important?"

She felt better for voicing her thoughts out loud. She would miss the social life of New Orleans, and Joe would probably never dress in anything other than buckskins. But finery no longer mattered. Being held in his arms was all that was important now.

Celia went to Faye and embraced her tenderly. "Then go to this man," she murmured. "And be happy for it, Faye. Nothing is more beautiful than being in love."

Faye returned the fond hug, then slipped away. She again eyed the gate through the window. Somehow the forest's depths did not frighten her. She could think only of Joe and that she would soon be in his embrace.

"*Oui*, nothing is more beautiful than being in love," she whispered, a sensual shiver coursing along her flesh.

She gave Celia a quick peck on her cheek, then swung the skirt of her dress around and hurried toward the foyer. "Remember, Celia, should anyone ask, I am in my room, embroidering," she said over her shoulder.

"I shall make sure Father Michael has no reason to wonder about you," Celia said, following Faye to the door.

Faye rushed to the stables and readied a horse and buggy, her fingers trembling anxiously. After climbing aboard, she rode from the mission.

She followed a narrow road that wound its way through the forest, having been told that this was the way to Joe's cabin. A short distance ahead there would be another road, and then, she hoped, there would be Joe....

Shirtless, Joe stood outside his cabin, leaning over a basin of water placed on a tree stump. Splashing the water onto his face, he grimaced in an effort to still the shiver brought on by the icy cold water.

Straightening, he dried his face and looked around him, enjoying this early June morning. The songbirds were singing their melodies, and a red-winged hawk soared above his head, carrying a field mouse in its claws.

Looking away from the sky, Joe slung the towel across his shoulder and dumped the water from the basin onto the ground. Then he went inside his cabin and pulled on his fringed shirt. Slinging his gun belt around his waist, positioning his long-barreled revolvers in place in their holsters, he went to the door and gazed outside.

His eyes followed Bart's arrival up the small lane that led to his front door. They had to go to the fort today and discuss affairs with Colonel Matthew Arbuckle, the commanding officer who was in charge of ridding the territory of tallow-whackers and out-laws.

So far it had been a losing battle. Father Michael had preached too often in favor of the vigilante movement for the arm of the law to do any good.

"Hey, there, Joe!" Bart said, reining his horse in close to the front door. "You don't know what you missed last night. Lordie, Joe, sometimes I don't know where your brain is."

Glowering, Joe pulled his front door closed, then swung himself up in his saddle. "Whenever I want a woman, I can damned well get one on my own. I don't need friends buying me an evening of fun in bed."

Bart laughed good-naturedly and rode off beside Joe, who had chosen to take a short-cut through the woods.

Her pulse racing, Faye spied Joe's cabin through the thick vegetation. She ducked as she rode beneath low-hanging limbs, then looked straight ahead again as she drew closer and closer to the cabin, her eyes anxious.

Drawing her buggy to a halt in front of Joe's cabin, she sat for a moment looking it over. It was a chink-and-daub log dwelling with a chimney at one end. Stacks of wood leaned against the stone chimney. Close by, an ax had been thrust into a thick stump.

In the yard beside the door, an iron washpot had been turned over near a round white spot on the ground where the wash water had been emptied. A basin was turned upside down on a stump close beside the washpot, the earth damp and wet beside it.

A surge of doubt gripped her, and she looked around wildly. There was no horse at the hitching post, and no movement within the cabin. Although it was early in the day, Joe was apparently gone.

Determined not to give up on seeing Joe, Faye climbed from the buggy. She secured her horse's reins and began walking slowly around the yard, giving Joe's cabin occasional glances.

So wanting to get a glimpse of Joe's life, Faye moved slowly toward the door. Her fingers trembled when she placed them on the latch and slowly raised it, and she jumped with a start when the door squeaked ominously as it began to creak open. Her eyes wide as she peered into the room now flooded by sunlight through the windows, Faye felt a strange sort of closeness to Joe when she stepped inside and began looking slowly around her.

The furniture was crude, obviously handmade, the tables a split slab on four legs set in auger holes. Three-legged stools were made in the same way.

Rough cupboards were built into one corner of the cabin, and a bed was at the far side, its outside rail a pole stuck into the wall and extending out into the room a foot or so above the floor. The loose end was supported by a forked leg.

Faye was discovering that the man she loved lived in even more primitive circumstances than she had ever imagined, yet perhaps all log cabins were furnished this way. Would Celia and Gayland's house be the same? Could Faye ever live like this?

Caught up in her discoveries, Faye forgot that she was intruding on Joe's privacy. Slowly, she moved about the cabin, touching things, familiarizing herself with them. Pegs were driven into one wall to hold clothes, and deer antlers hung over the door for a gun rack.

Whirling around, she once more began to walk slowly about the room, crossing the puncheon floor, her eyes shifting from item to item. Then she stopped cold in her tracks when she spied something that she had not seen earlier. She paled as she moved closer to it, then with trembling fingers she knelt down before a trunk that stood behind a table and touched a dress that had been casually thrown across it.

Numb, she fingered the ivory gown with English net, scoop neckline, puff sleeves and full skirt. Pearl beading and wide alençon lace accented the wedding gown.

Clapping her palm over her mouth, she fought to stifle a sob, jealousy stinging her insides. She lifted the dress, not wanting to admire its loveliness, but unable to help but see it as one of the most beautiful she had ever seen. It begged to be worn, and Faye could not help but want to try it on. Since she had left New Orleans, she had missed the fun of going to shops and choosing, then trying on dresses.

Dropping the dress as though it were a hot coal, Faye rose quickly to her feet, angry with Joe for having toyed with her affections. All along there had been a woman. A marriage was surely planned, or why else would there be a wedding dress in his cabin?

Moving back to her knees before the trunk, Faye lifted the dress into her arms once again. Though it belonged to another, she still wanted to try it on. What could it hurt?

Taking the wedding dress and placing it across the bed, Faye hurried to strip down to her petticoat. Her heart thumping wildly, she slipped the gown over her head and fastened it.

Stepping into the light at the window where the sun streamed in, she ran her fingers over the softness of the material where it fitted her so snugly at the waist.

Then when she heard the sound of an approaching horse, she sucked in her breath with sudden fright. Her fingers fumbling, she tried to unhook the dress from behind, all the while watching the door. Blood rushed to her face, and her eyes widened. She had come to this cabin to see Joe, and now it was apparent that she *was* going to in only a moment.

Chapter Fifteen

Taking a shaky step backward, Faye jumped with alarm when the door swung open widely, revealing Joe standing there. Faye scarcely breathed as he raked his eyes over her. Looking at her with venom in his eyes, he stomped toward her.

"Take off that dress," he ordered flatly, towering over her.

Faye just looked at him, too numb to move. She cried out softly when his fingers roughly tore the hooks apart before he briskly pulled the dress over her head.

Suddenly she found herself standing in only her petticoat while Joe still glared down at her. The wedding dress had been tossed aside on a table.

"Dammit, Faye," he said hoarsely. "What's going on here? I return to my cabin because I forget my rifle and find you here trying on that dress. Why?"

Tears pooled in Faye's eyes, feeling as though she had been stripped naked. Humiliated, she drew her arms across her heaving breasts, fighting the urge to cry.

Joe let out a pent-up breath and with a curse turned away. This was not the time to question why she did anything. Wasn't it enough that she had cared enough for him to find out where he lived and come to him? Surely she had not expected him to be gone so early in the day, and she had damned well not expected to find another lady's dress among his belongings.

"I'm sorry," Faye murmured, blinking tears from her eyelashes. "I know I shouldn't have come. I especially shouldn't have entered your house while you were gone." She began to inch toward her clothes that lay across the bed. "I shall be gone as quickly as I can get dressed."

"Faye, no," Joe said, whipping back around. "I didn't mean to be so abrupt with you. It's just that it was such a surprise to find you here in such a way." He laughed throatily as he gripped her arms and began to draw her closer. "Last night I could barely sleep for worrying about how I could manage to get you away from your brother, and now here you are. I'm damned grateful, Faye."

"Grateful for what?" she asked dryly. "That I come to you to give myself to you so willingly again? Is that all you want from me, Joe? Is that all you ever wanted of me?"

Joe's eyes widened, and he swallowed hard. "You know that's not so," he said hoarsely. "You know that I love you."

Faye glanced over at the dress. "I find that hard to believe," she said, almost choking on a sob. "If you truly love me, why do you have another woman's wedding dress in your house?"

Joe's mind began to swirl, trying to grasp on to some sort of truth that would make Faye understand and not hurt her, yet there was none. To explain about another woman who was first in his heart would chance devastating Faye and any feelings that she had for him. The fact that he hadn't burned the dress was hardly understood by him. How could he expect her to understand?

There could be no truths about the dress. There could only be lies. For now, anyhow. When he had claimed Faye as totally his, then he would explain. Then the hurt would be less, for he would have proved his love to her by making her his wife!

"The dress?" he said, his voice faltering. Quickly, he searched his mind for a good reason. He could not tell Faye the truth. The truth would only send her running. "It was my cousin's. She left it and her trunk with me when she and her husband left on a trip south. There wasn't room for everything in the wagon they were traveling in. You understand that, for you more than likely had to leave many of your beloved belongings back in New Orleans."

Faye studied his eyes, sensing a lie as sure as she was standing there. She wanted to believe him, for she ached to be in his arms.

"Faye?" Joe said, drawing her into his arms. His mouth moved to her lips. "You haven't said anything. Can't you see I'm sorry? Tell me that I'm forgiven."

Faye strained against him, pushing against his chest with her hands. Passion was weakening her defenses as his eyes burned down into hers. His lips were so close that she was becoming dizzy with need.

"Joe, don't," Faye murmured, trembling uncontrollably when his tongue swept across her lips sensually.

"You find it so hard to forgive me?" Joe said huskily, holding her imprisoned within his muscled arms. His gaze swept over her face. "Let me make it all up to you. Let me make love to you."

"Oh, Joe, do you think that is the solution to everything?" Faye cried softly, her breath faltering when he reached a hand between them and cupped a breast. She closed her eyes, ecstasy taking hold in bone-weakening intensity. "Joe, please don't. I ... must ... go...."

"No, you mustn't," he whispered, feathering kisses across her face. "You can't want to, Faye."

When he reached down beneath her petticoat to take her breast into his hand, to softly knead it,

Faye's attempts to pull away waned. She looked up at him, and her eyes filled with passion.

"I had to come," she murmured, her hair cascading across her bare shoulders as she lifted her lips close to his. "Oh, Joe, I heard you and Michael quarreling last night. By the time I got to the foyer, you were already gone. I have come to apologize for my brother's crudeness. I have come to thank you for returning my shawl."

She parted her lips with a sigh as he kissed the hollow of her throat. "I have come because I now know how impossible my brother is going to make it for you and me to be together," she whispered. "Oh, Joe, what is it between the two of you? Why do you detest each other so?"

Joe slipped his hand from her breast. His powerful arms pulled her closer against his hard frame. He kissed her brow, then her eyes, then ran his tongue across her lips.

"This isn't the time to discuss your brother," he whispered. "Or anything else, for that matter. Darling, you are here. I need you. And you need me. I see it in your eyes." He bent his head and placed his lips beneath her left breast. "I feel it in the way your heart beats so soundly against my lips!"

"But you returned to your cabin to get your rifle," Faye murmured, her breath stolen away when he swept her up into his arms and began carrying her toward his bed. "Surely you had other plans. I am only in the way."

"Never," Joe said huskily, placing her on his bed beside her clothes. Gently he took her dress and draped it over a stool, then went back to the bed to stand over her. "What I had planned for this morning can be done just as easily this afternoon. And that might not even be necessary. Bart rode on ahead to the fort. Perhaps he can see to everything this time without me."

Kneeling beside the bed, Joe slowly began to lower Faye's delicate underthings, leaving a trail of kisses behind, igniting fires along her willing flesh. She quivered with ecstasy when his mouth closed over her breast and his tongue flicked the nipple into a hard peak. She moaned lightly when his lips moved lower to where she so painfully ached between the thighs.

Sucking in her breath, Faye twined her fingers through Joe's thick mane of black hair and drew his mouth closer. She whimpered as the wondrous feelings of bliss mounted, blocking out all sense of time and thought. She was with Joe.

When Joe crept away from her and stood over her to remove his clothes, Faye moved from the bed and placed his hands down to his side. "Let me," she said softly. Her fingers trembled as she placed her hands at the fringed hem of his shirt and began pulling it up across his chest. As she drew it over his head, she leaned toward him and flicked her tongue across one of his nipples, knowing that he enjoyed it by his soft gasp.

The shirt tossed aside, Faye moved her tongue downward, leaving a heated trail in its wake. Her fingers lowered his breeches until they dropped in a heap around his ankles. When she saw his swollen manhood, she coiled her fingers around him, all the while looking into his eyes, watching the passion mounting in their fathomless, dark depths.

Joe clasped her shoulders and guided her back to the bed, arranging her beneath him, devouring her with his eyes. "Enough of that," he said, laughing huskily. "You're making me mindless much too quickly." His hands caressed her silken flesh as he began softly probing with his hardness between her thighs. "Darling, when I'm with you, I want the real thing." He kissed her softly. "I want you, Faye. All of you."

Faye moaned softly as he entered her and began his strokes within her, awakening her to feelings that had been dormant since she had last been with him in such a way. Pleasure spread through her body, and a raging hunger overcame her as she clung to him and tasted his lips. His hands eagerly searched her body, then claimed her secret place as his.

She drew a ragged breath when he cupped a breast and kneaded it until the pleasure became intermixed with a sweet sort of pain. The hot touch of his body against hers, the way his lean, sinewy buttocks moved in such a steady rhythm, made the heat of passion burn higher. She grew feverish as he cradled her even more closely.

Joe groaned huskily as he felt the tightness in his loins coil intensely as he moved within her slowly and deliberately. His tongue brushed her lips lightly, his eyes dark and stormy as he gazed down at her.

"Kiss me ... hold me," she whispered, her ankles locked about him as his lips bore down upon her in a savage kiss.

When he moved, she moved. When the pleasure began to peak for one, it did for the other. They clung and rocked together as that ultimate of joy was reached and savored.

"I'm so glad that I came to be with you," Faye whispered, running her fingers over his dampened chest hairs. "Oh, Joe, I don't want to leave! I love you with such a gentle passion. You love me the same. I can tell."

He turned to her, his hand making a slow, sensuous descent along her spine as he looked down at her, his face a mask of naked desire. "I do love you the same," he said, his voice deep and resonant. "Must you leave? Stay with me. Be my woman. Now and forevermore!"

His words caught Faye off guard. She drew away from him, alarm registering in her eyes. "Stay with you?" she gasped. "Joe, how do you mean? You don't mean before marriage vows are spoken, do you?''

Joe studied her expression, then rose from the bed and pulled on his breeches. ''Of course you couldn't do that,'' he growled. ''Your brother would never allow it.'' He swung around and glowered down at her. ''He and I have had too many differences for him to ever give a marriage between you and me any sort of a blessing.''

Faye looked up at him, dismayed at Joe for speaking of marriage to her in one breath and hate for her brother in another.

Rising slowly from the bed, going to Joe to ease into his arms, Faye looked up at him and implored him with her eyes. ''What do you want of me?'' she murmured. ''You weren't serious when you spoke of me just living casually with you, were you? You know that I was brought up with stronger morals than that. That I have given myself to you before marriage has gone against all that I was ever taught. But I love you so much I could not help myself. Yet I cannot live openly with you if I am not your wife. If you love me, surely you won't ask that of me.''

Joe's gaze moved slowly over her as though in a caress, seeing her as perfect in every way. He bent his lips to a breast and drew a nipple between his lips and flicked his tongue around it, smiling to himself as he listened to her moan sensually.

Then he stepped away from her and picked up her clothes and placed them in her arms. "Darling, you had better get dressed or I'll not be able to keep my hands or my lips off you," he said, laughing softly.

He went to a window and gazed from it as she dressed quietly behind him. Perhaps now *was* the time to warn her about her brother! Perhaps now was the time for him to trust Faye completely. If he couldn't do it now, maybe never.

Joe momentarily hung his head.

Faye hurried into the rest of her clothes, then looked at Joe with an ache in her heart. His silence was such a sad one. Longing to give comfort, Faye went to Joe and stood in front of him, placing herself between him and the window. Twining her arms about his neck, she looked up at him and smiled. "I did as you asked," she murmured. "I got dressed. Now what do you have on your mind, Joe Harrison?"

Joe gazed down at her with longing. "Faye, we need to talk," he said thickly. He motioned toward two chairs opposite the fireplace. "Let's go sit down. I've much to explain to you."

Faye grew tense, the seriousness of the moment unnerving her. She returned his gaze momentarily, then nodded and walked alongside him and sat down on the wooden chair. Joe turned the other one so that he would face her. Taking her hands, he leaned close to her.

"Faye, there's been some bad blood between me and your brother for some time," he said, clearing his throat nervously when he saw her eyes take on a pained look. He held more tightly to her hands as she tried to move away from him. "Hear me out. It's best for all concerned if you do. All right?"

Her spine stiff, the pit of her stomach strangely empty, Faye nodded and tried to relax. *"Oui,"* she murmured. "Do go on."

Joe's eyes were fathomlessly dark as he peered into Faye's. "Your brother and I, well, we have many differences of opinions about many things," he continued. "One is how law should be enforced in these parts. I believe in the need for an orderly government to enforce the law and keep peace. Your brother is in direct conflict with my beliefs. He preaches more than religion. He antagonizes and incites people into joining with those who are members of a vigilance committee. Father Michael believes everyone has the right to take the law into his own hands the way they had been forced to when the mission was first established in this area as a haven for settlers. Fort Smith was built several years later. Father Michael can't accept that those who are in command at the fort are now the law, not the vigilantes."

He paused and searched Faye's face, now seeing confusion in her eyes. "Your brother asked me to join forces with those of the committee," he added hurriedly. "They wanted me because of my skills with my gun. I refused. Now do you see why there is so much tension between me and your brother? Can you see how wrong he is?" He laughed throatily. "A man of God inciting violence? Even you are in danger while you are living beneath the same roof as he. One of these days the outlaws are going to seek revenge, and your brother will be one of their first targets. They know that he helps the vigilantes. I'm damned surprised he isn't one himself."

Stunned, Faye stared blankly into Joe's eyes, finding the truth hard to comprehend. Michael? A priest who preached violence? Michael? The gentle man with a heart of gold who spread sunshine to so many in need?

Jerking her hands from Joe's, Faye rose, stumbling in her haste. "No," she insisted, "it can't be. Not Michael. He's a priest...a man of God. You must be wrong, Joe!"

She went to Joe and pummeled her fists against his powerful chest. "Tell me you're wrong!" she cried. "My brother is so kind...so gentle!"

Joe took Faye by her wrists and drew her close to him. "Faye, you have always thought of him as saintly because he is a priest," he said hoarsely. "You will always be blinded to the truth unless you listen to me now and accept it."

His tone softened as he leaned down toward her face. "And, darling," he tried to reassure her, "it's not the end of the world just because your brother is driven to make things right. I can see why he does it. So why can't you? It's just that understanding his motives does not make his actions right, or make me accept him any more readily. I can't now, nor shall I ever. It's just that you needed to know and realize that your best place is with me."

Drawing her close, he pressed his cheek to her brow. "My darling, marry me," he said scarcely above a whisper. "Leave your brother. Even today!"

Torn, Faye squirmed from his embrace. "As I see it, you want me only so that you can get back at my brother," she accused him, choking back a sob. "Can't you ever be sincere, Joe Harrison?"

With that she grabbed the wedding dress and turning back to Joe, threw it into his face. "And as for your tale of the dress, I didn't believe it for a minute!" she stormed.

Faye's heart stopped when Joe pulled the dress away to reveal a face so dark with anger that she hardly recognized it as his. His eyes were lit with fire. He threw the dress over his shoulder and took a wide step toward her.

Suddenly the door flew open and Bart burst into the cabin, winded, his face dripping with perspiration.

"Joe, come quick!" Bart shouted, stopping and staring from Joe to Faye when he discovered that Joe wasn't alone.

"Bart, what the...?" Joe said, but was interrupted when Bart collected himself.

"I didn't get to the fort," he said anxiously. "I saw fire in the distance. The damned outlaws had set fire to the Stafford place and had stolen their horses. Joe, we'd best get after them unless we're already too late. Those thieves seem to disappear into thin air. So do the horses they always steal!"

Faye gave Joe a lingering stare, torn between loyalties to him and her brother, then turned on a heel and rushed from the cabin. Not heeding Joe's insistence that he escort her home, she grabbed the horse's reins and pulled herself up into the driver's seat. With a cruel crack of the whip, she headed away from him, maybe forever.

Chapter Sixteen

Faye stood at the parlor window of the rectory watching Celia and the children who sat outside at her feet on the ground beneath a willow tree. Celia had been instantly taken by the children who traveled from far and wide to attend school at the mission, and each evening before they all returned home, she gathered them together and read books to them. Faye's heart warmed, glad that Celia had, in a sense, finally found children to call her own, if only for a few moments in the afternoons.

Her attention was averted when Michael rode into view on his horse-drawn buckboard wagon as he guided it through the open gates. She drew the curtain aside to get a better look at her brother, Joe's accusations troubling her. What he had said must have been true, for why would Joe lie?

But how could Michael, the holy man he was, preach violence?

Faye's eyes followed Michael as he climbed from the wagon and stood still, silently observing Celia and the children whose eyes were intent on her as she turned another page in her book. He then went from child to child, patting each on the head. Their adoring, trusting eyes looked up at him. Maybe it was Michael's love of children that prompted him to do what he felt was best to protect them.

Tensing, Faye let the curtain flutter back in place when Michael glanced toward the window. Slowly she turned and waited for his entry into the parlor, not knowing what she would say to him.

The sound of footsteps drawing near made Faye straighten her back and square her shoulders. She smiled awkwardly at Michael as he entered the room, his black robe swooshing as he ambled toward her.

"How was your day?" Michael asked, going to Faye to give her a warm hug.

"It was fine," she said, confused, not knowing whether to return the hug since she no longer absolutely knew this man.

But filled with such love for him, her arms slowly lifted, and she twined them around him and hugged him for all it was worth. No matter his ideals, he was her brother, and she loved him.

Michael hugged her more closely and patted her back, then stepped away from her. He took her hands and held them, looking down into her eyes. "I at first felt something lacking in your hug," he said softly. "What is it?" His jaw tightened and his eyes narrowed. "Did that army scout come by and pester you again? If so, I'll..."

The approach of a horse outside abruptly took Michael's attention away from her. Dropping her hands, he went to the window and lifted the curtain to glare outside.

"No, the scout was surely not here earlier, for he has just arrived *now*," Michael said, his tone cool and measured. He let the curtain flutter back in place and turned to face Faye. "It seems you have made quite an impression on that man. Before you arrived from New Orleans, he never showed his face around here at all."

Faye's eyes widened and her knees grew suddenly weak. "Joe?" she gasped. "He's here?"

"That name is spoken so familiarly by you," Michael said, his eyes wavering. "Faye, why?"

A loud slamming of the door and heavy footsteps drew Faye to look past Michael. Joe Harrison stormed fiercely into the room, his eyes wild. With long strides, he paced across the heavy Indian rugs, stopping directly in front of Michael.

"I have but two things to say to you," Joe announced menacingly, moving his face closer to Michael's. "First to tell you that Faye is going to marry me no matter what you say about it, and second, I want you to know that Bart and I just caught two of the outlaws responsible for burning the Stafford place and stealing their horses. The men are now in the guardhouse at the fort where they belong, awaiting a legal trial. They are not hanging from a tree. I've proved to you today just how the outlaws should be dealt with. If law and order is to be had in the community, placing the outlaws behind bars is the way it should be done, Father Michael, whether or not you will ever agree.''

Michael's face had turned a deep red with anger. He grimaced forcefully in an effort to compose himself. ''So you caught two of the outlaws,'' he said dryly. ''What of the others? Of course they run rampant across the land, eluding everyone. The army's interferences have not made it any better in these parts. The vigilantes have the right to take law into their own hands. Bringing outlaws in two at a time won't work, Joe.''

He clasped a hand to Joe's shoulder. Faye saw Joe wince at the gesture.

''Joe, join forces with the vigilantes,'' Michael said softly. ''As I said before, they need your skills with your gun. If you were able to round up two of the outlaws today with just Bart Dobbs helping you, imagine what could be done if you worked with a group of vigilantes. This area could be cleaned up in no time flat. You can do more good for the community by working with the vigilantes than being a scout for the army.''

Joe casually moved Michael's hand from his shoulder. "We've been over this before," he growled. "You're wasting your time. I'm not someone who listens to what you preach."

Michael frowned and kneaded his brow. "You're as stubborn as a mule," he said sourly. "You're as fed up with the outlaws terrorizing the settlers as I am, yet you won't take the steps necessary to correct it."

Faye grimaced when Joe leaned into Michael's face, speaking between clenched teeth.

"Father Michael, why can't you just tend to preaching and leave the law to the lawmakers?" he said, a warning in his tone. "You're risking many innocent lives by encouraging people to take the law into their own hands, including the lives of everyone at the mission."

"You don't know what you're talking about," Michael said, stepping back. He went to the window and gazed out at the children still intently listening to Celia. "No place is safer than here. No place."

Joe moved to Michael's side. "Faye isn't safe here, and I'm going to remedy that," he said, giving her a glance. "Father Michael, whether or not you give Faye your blessing, she's going to marry me."

Stunned, Faye watched mutely, having not once been brought into the conversation. She was not about to be bartered for between the two most stubborn men she knew.

Taking several quick steps toward Michael and Joe, she positioned herself between them. "Do I have anything to say about anything, or am I looked to as just a mere woman whose opinions matter not at all?" she fumed. Placing her hands on her hips, she looked up into Joe's fathomless eyes. "Joe, you have come to tell Michael you are going to marry me. Don't you think it would be best to see if I now even want to marry you? As I see it, there is much left unsettled between us."

"Yes, I imagine there is," Michael interjected. "Joe, did you tell Faye about Kathryn yet? Did you tell Faye that she walked out on you just prior to your wedding day? But, no, I doubt if you told her that. It would give Faye cause to believe that you have chosen her only to heal your broken heart. Faye is second choice, *isn't* she, Joe?"

The color drained from Faye's face as she looked from Joe to Michael, and then back to Joe. Her brother's words had torn her heart to shreds. She felt numb as she witnessed Joe's drawn expression.

Now she understood. The wedding dress had belonged to a woman Joe had planned to marry—a woman who had walked out on him.

"Joe, I can't ask you to deny this," Faye said, choking back a sob. "It's all true, isn't it? The wedding dress I found in your cabin? It belonged to a woman named Kathryn!"

Abruptly, Michael placed a hand to Faye's wrist and swung her around, frowning down at her. "What did you say?" he gasped. "You were in Joe's cabin? Faye, why would you go there, unless..."

Faye jerked her wrist free. Tears began streaming down her burning cheeks. "Don't say another thing," she cried. "Michael, haven't you already said enough?"

She lifted the hem of her dress and ran from the room. At the sound of footsteps behind her, she half stumbled as she reached the foot of the staircase. Using the banister to steady herself, she hurried on up the stairs and to her room, ignoring Joe's protests behind her.

Closing her bedroom door and locking it, she leaned her back against it. Never had she cried so hard. Joe's words stung her heart as he pleaded from outside the door. Then she heard Michael's loud, distinctive voice ordering Joe from the house. She sobbed into her hands when Joe cursed Michael, and, in a softer voice, again began talking to Faye through the closed door.

"Faye, it's not at all the way Michael said," Joe said softly, again rattling the doorknob in hopes of springing the lock. "Sure Kathryn left before we got married. But I didn't choose you just to take her place. When I met you, I fell in love in a much different way than with Kathryn. You're special. You're sweet. Please listen to me, darling. I love you for *you*."

"Now I understand so much," Faye sobbed, sniffling into her palm as she wiped her nose and eyes. "You ran hot and cold with me. You still do! It's because you are comparing me with this woman. You say that I'm different. In truth, it was a difference you did not enjoy! Go away, Joe Harrison. Go away!"

"Faye, you're wrong," Joe pleaded. "I pulled away from you when you doubted yourself and your abilities to cope. You see, Kathryn was a city woman, too. That's why she returned home. She couldn't tolerate living in the wilderness and all the inconveniences of that sort of life. I . . . couldn't . . . bear it if you would love, then leave me, also. A man can take only so much rejection, Faye."

"Well, you had better get used to it," Faye cried, her jaw tightening. "I never want to see you again. Not only am I second choice for you, but you also lied to me. You could not tell me the truth about Kathryn's wedding dress. How can I believe anything that you are saying now? Go away, Joe." With that, she stifled a sob behind her hand. "Just . . . leave . . . me be."

Joe doubled a fist and slammed it against the door, his blood boiling. "I was right about you all along!" he shouted. "You are a stubborn, spoiled woman. I'm glad I got my eyes opened soon enough. Lord help me if I had taken you as my wife. I poured my heart out to you to get you to understand; and you won't listen. I lied about the dress only to save hurtful feelings, but now I don't care about how you feel about anything. You can stay here with your precious brother and rot for all I care!''

His angry words made Faye's insides splash cold. She couldn't believe that things were going to end like this. How could she lose a man she loved so dearly? But her pride had been hurt and perhaps could never be repaired. All the while Joe had been holding her in his arms he had more than likely been seeing this woman Kathryn in his mind's eye!

Oh, how it hurt her to think that.

Faye collapsed against the door and listened as Joe shouted at Michael as he stormed down the staircase.

''Father Michael, I didn't think I'd ever have you to thank for anything!'' Joe shouted. ''But I'm thanking you now for forcing me to see just the sort your sister is. Maybe one of your vigilante friends will want to take her off your hands. Think so?''

Joe's boisterous laughter echoed through the rectory and through Faye's closed door. She cringed away from the door, and heading for her bed, crumpled down on it.

Chapter Seventeen

The forest echoed the ring of the axes as the men cleared the land. Everyone from miles around had arrived to join in the house-raising for Celia and Gayland, not only to help their new neighbor, but also to spend some time with their neighbors and catch up with everyone's news.

In a portion of the cleared land, Faye moved among the women around a great outdoor fire, helping prepare the food for the noon and evening meals. In her dress with puffed sleeves and full skirt over a lace-trimmed petticoat, she was learning the art of making pot pie, the standard dish at all house-raisings. Squash, pumpkin, potatoes and cabbage were being added to turkey as it cooked in a heavy iron pot. Later they would put in enough dumplings for everyone.

"Isn't this a wonderful thing everyone is doing for us?" Celia asked, stepping to Faye's side and adding sliced cabbage to the large pot. Her green eyes were anxious and wide as she looked over at Faye, her pale green cotton dress neatly tucked at the waist. "They say by dusk the house will be finished. It's all so grand!"

Faye did not want to spoil Celia's day by revealing that she was less than cheerful about anything. A week had passed since the terrible scene with Joe and Michael, a week in which she had not been able to sleep.

Faye smiled over at Celia. "*Oui*, I'm very happy for you," she murmured, then tensed as she heard Joe's voice over that of the other men.

She wanted to turn and look at him but was afraid to. She didn't want their eyes to meet. He would see so much in hers that she did not want to reveal.

Celia dropped the last of the cabbage into the boiling liquid. She laid her knife aside and wiped her hands on her skirt, watching the other women set up the wooden frames in the shade for the quilting bee.

"Faye, you will be quilting with us women, won't you?" she asked excitedly. "There's not much else to do with preparing the meal until time to serve it."

She grabbed Faye's arm as Faye placed her knife aside. "Come on," she encouraged softly. "Take a seat beside me."

Glad to have something to keep her from looking at Joe, Faye walked with Celia toward the women who were busy readying themselves for a day of sewing. Benches had been placed around a massive frame now covered by a ten-foot-square pieces of cotton fabric. Faye watched as the women then laid down the batting, and then the colorful top piece.

As the rest of the women settled themselves on the benches around the fabric-covered frame, Celia guided Faye to a corner where they took a seat. Soon a needle was placed in her hand, and after watching how the others wove the thread in and out of the fabric in small stitches, she took a few practice stitches of her own. It didn't take long for her to catch on.

"See?" Celia said as Faye had to stop to thread her needle with a new piece. "Didn't I say that it would be enjoyable?"

The women began gossiping and laughing among themselves. The focus of a house-raising as far as the women were concerned was socializing in the way it was done in the Ozarks—quilting now, dancing later.

"Faye, maybe one day there will be a house-raising for you," Celia said, drawing the needle through the cotton material. She glanced over at Joe, then at Faye. "Honey, you're so quiet today. Perhaps you can make up with Joe? It's just a lovers' quarrel. That's all."

"No, it's not all that simple," Faye said, pulling her needle through the layers of fabric, wincing when she pricked her finger. "There's too much that I haven't told you, Celia. I believe too much irreparable harm has been done. I don't want to ever speak with Joe Harrison again. He's an arrogant, deceitful man.''

Celia brushed a loose tendril of hair back from her brow. "Faye, I must admit something to you," Celia said in a whisper, leaning close to her. "Gayland heard everything that happened the day when Joe and Michael had such a terrible argument.''

Celia looked solemn. "I'm sorry, Faye," she murmured, "but maybe you're being too hard on Joe. If there was another woman in his life, she's long gone. And don't most men and women love more than once in a lifetime? If Joe is the first for you, you are lucky.''

Faye turned her eyes slowly to Celia. "Celia, are you saying that Gayland wasn't the first man in your life?" she asked in a shocked whisper. "There was someone else? You and Gayland seem so totally devoted!''

Celia lowered her eyes, focusing her attention on the design taking shape on the quilt. "A long time ago there was a boy," she said softly. "Yes, a boy. He was seventeen, I was sixteen. We were madly in love. We sneaked away and met as often as we could by the riverbank in Kentucky. At first we only kissed and held hands. Then one day it went further.'' She swallowed hard. "My parents found out when I became pregnant. By then the boy and his family had moved from the area so I could not marry him. But I lost the child, anyhow.''

She turned misty eyes back to Faye. "So you see?" she said thinly, "though I loved deeply before I met Gayland, I could never love as dearly and completely as now."

She reached over and patted Faye's hand. "Honey, it is surely the same with Joe. I have seen it in the way he looks at you. He is not seeing another woman when he looks at you. How could he?" She laughed softly. "No other woman could be as pretty and as sweet. Honey, Joe loves you for you. Love him back. Don't wait for a second time around for you, for sometimes it doesn't happen. Out here in this wilderness, most men already have wives. They move here as families."

Celia frowned. "Well, the soldiers are quite unattached, but hardly eligible. They cannot appreciate refinement, so they spend their nights in the saloons," she said, giving Joe a quick glance. "Never again will you find a man like Joe Harrison. He's proved his worth to us all. He's proved to be quite a charitable, likable man!"

Faye was touched by Celia's caring, and she wanted to believe everything that her friend said about Joe. But she had grown too wary to let her guard down.

Daring to, she looked his way and felt the familiar warmth spread through her. He had removed his shirt. His neck was muscular and tanned, his sun-bronzed back and chest rippling with muscles as he helped the men build the house.

Faye could not deny that watching him was causing her heart to pound, but she could not draw her eyes away. His mere presence mesmerized her. It was as though she was looking at him for the very first time. His shoulder-length raven-black hair had been drawn back and tied by a leather thong, his face was pearling with sweat under the hot rays of the sun. His dark, fathomless eyes were proud and sure as he glanced over at her, catching her watching him.

Blushing, Faye turned her eyes away and focused on her sewing.

"Faye, did you hear anything I said?" Celia asked, exasperated. "Perhaps tonight when everyone is dancing, you might allow Joe to dance with you. Please think about it seriously, Faye. Life is too short to go through it lonesome and heartbroken. Let Joe fill the gap in your life left by the death of your parents. I assure you, marriage is the answer for many things." Celia blushed. "The nights are heavenly, Faye," she whispered. "Just heavenly."

Faye glanced quickly over at Celia, then smiled softly when she recalled the precious moments Celia and Gayland had stolen on the trail. Then she looked slowly over at Joe, recalling their own stolen moments. If she allowed herself, she could even now feel the touch of his hands on her body, the teasing and tormenting of his lips.

She set her jaw firmly, glaring at Joe as he joked casually with the men, as though not at all bothered by the circumstances that had drawn him away from Faye. If he was bothered at all by her absence, he did not show it.

"No, I won't dance with that man tonight or ever," Faye blurted angrily. "Please don't speak of him to me again."

Her lips clamped stubbornly tight, she let her needle grow idle and forced herself to watch Joe, hoping that he would look her way and see that she was not affected by him, either! She would show him in one way or the other that she cared nothing for him.

But, busy with the task at hand, Joe did not look back. The trees had been felled, the logs trimmed, notched at the ends and then fitted into place. Thin wedges of wood had been inserted where the logs did not fit. The cracks were being daubed with a mixture of clay, grass and mud. Joe was hard at work on the roof, aligning the poles over a simple frame.

"Faye, you've stopped sewing," Celia said, drawing Faye from her reverie. "Aren't you enjoying yourself?"

Faye's gaze was drawn back to the pattern taking place on the fabric. The women were still working diligently with their threads and needles.

Embarrassed, Faye resumed her sewing, nodding to Celia's incessant chatterings, wishing that she could be as content. Celia had everything in life, it seemed, except a child, and she had learned to accept that one misfortune. Perhaps Faye could learn to live with her own misfortunes.

"Soon it will be time to stop to feed the men," Celia said, glancing over at Gayland. "The men will stop long enough to have some fun." She giggled, nudging Faye with an elbow. "It wouldn't be fair if we women had all the fun, now would it?"

Faye smiled awkwardly. "No, not fair at all," she murmured. She wanted to say that nothing seemed to be fair where men were concerned, but she kept her troubled thoughts to herself.

Catching herself again looking at Joe longingly, Faye held her breath as he suddenly turned toward her, imploring her with his midnight black eyes, his jaw set tightly. She wanted so to smile at him, give him some sort of encouragement, but her pride won out.

"Damn you, Joe Harrison," she whispered beneath her breath so that no one could hear.

For a moment, an angry fire lit up his eyes. Then he turned on his heel and stomped off into the forest with a group of men to haul more logs into the clearing.

Faye resumed her sewing, and it did not seem long at all before the women began laying their thread and needles aside to go and spread blankets across the ground in the shade. Chattering and laughing, they served up the food on large platters and filled and refilled the tin cups with freshly brewed coffee. The men left their work and ate ravenously, enjoying the lunch and a well-earned leisurely noon hour in the shade as the women continued to pile their plates high with pot pie.

Then after the women had also eaten and time had come for fun and games, Faye stepped back away from the crowd and watched quietly from the edge of the clearing. The men and boys challenged each other with tomahawk throws, races and wrestling matches. They then matched their skills as marksmen. Faye moved closer to the area squared off for the shooting match. Her pulse raced as Joe gave her occasional glances, and her eyes followed the movement of his bare chest and shoulder muscles as he cut a piece of bark from a tree. Then using a little powder whetted with saliva, he marked a bull's-eye on it. In the fork of a different tree, he set a bleached buffalo skull for a second target.

Lining up, the men aimed with their pistols and took turns firing at the targets. Joe was the only one who got a bull's-eye as he shot square through the eye socket of the buffalo skull. And he was the only one who over and over again hit the bull's-eye on the piece of bark.

Faye couldn't help but smile sheepishly at him when he gave her a smile as he stood blowing smoke from his revolver. Though he had shown off like a young schoolboy, she could not help but admire his abilities with the pistol, and regretted that he still could affect her in such a way.

But there was no denying that he did. She was very relieved when the games were over and the men were back at work and the women were once again sitting around the quilt that was taking shape in the afternoon shade.

Chapter Eighteen

The sun was beginning to set, shading the distant hills in purple and gray. A breeze sighed in the grass, rustling the leaves of the cottonwoods. Celia and Gayland's log cabin stood bold and new in the clearing, the last stone having just been set in the fireplace.

"Can you believe that they got the cabin built in one day?" Celia marveled, sighing as she clasped her hands eagerly before her. "And isn't it beautiful, Faye?"

Celia's gaze swept over the cabin, seeing it as nothing less than perfect, even though no windowpanes had been installed. The ones they had ordered were on their way from New Orleans, but a buckskin covering would do for now.

At the pride in Celia's voice, Faye tried to look at the cabin as something wonderful, and though it was brand-new, she could see nothing that grand about it. In her mind's eye she was recalling the mansion that she had been raised in. Nothing would ever compare with it. She missed it. She missed her friends who had always come to call. And she missed her parents.

And if she had married Joe Harrison, a crude cabin would have been her home. But the thought of living with him there had not been all that intolerable—she would have been living with the man she loved.

So it was the same with Celia. She and Gayland's special love for each other would make the drabness of the cabin glow.

"*Oui*, it's wonderful," Faye said in a rush, hugging Celia fondly.

At the sound of a fiddle tuning up, Faye turned toward the slight rise of land at the side of the house where everyone was congregating around a roaring bonfire. Soon the dancing would begin, and her heart beat wildly as she saw Joe move along the outer fringes of the crowd, laughing and joking with everyone, patting the other men on their backs.

Faye's gaze swept over Joe. Fresh and clean, he must have bathed in the creek along with the rest of the men. His hair was once again hanging loose to his shoulders, black and shining sleekly.

When Joe turned his eyes on her, she stiffened, yet had no control over the thundering of her heart or of the weakness that invaded her knees.

"Faye, remember what I said," Celia murmured, circling Faye's hand with one of her own as she saw the longing in her friend's eyes. "Life's too short. Don't let pride stand in the way of the love you have for that man. Go to him. Go to him now."

Faye felt Joe's eyes branding her, burning a path of desire clean to her heart. She felt herself being drawn to him as always before, but this time she could not allow it.

Easing her hand from Celia's, Faye turned her back to Joe. "I can't," she choked, and shook her head despairingly. "I . . . just . . . can't."

Celia patted Faye's arm. "Well, perhaps not now," she said softly. "Maybe later. The night will be long. I have been told by the other ladies that there will be dancing until the sun rises in the morning."

"There will be dancing all night?" Faye gasped, all hope of returning to the mission dashed.

Celia once again patted Faye on the arm. "All night," she said, giggling. She gave Gayland a wistful stare as he mingled with the men. "Now let's join in the fun, shall we?"

"Yes, let's," Faye said, firming her jaw and lifting her chin stubbornly as she felt Joe watching her every movement. She walked along with Celia, thinking that surely this would be the longest night of her life, especially if Joe insisted that she dance with him. If she was held only once within his wondrous arms again, she would be lost to him forever.

"Faye, you are going to dance, aren't you?" Gayland asked, moving to Celia's side and draping an arm around her waist. His bald head was peeling from a fresh sunburn, and his nose was crimson. He nodded toward a banjo tuning up beside the fiddler. "Soon the hills will be ringing with the banjo and fiddle. It'll make you want to dance, hon."

Faye looked at Joe over her shoulder, knowing that if she joined in the square dancing, she could not help but have him for an occasional partner. She moved her eyes back to Gayland and placed a hand to her brow. "Perhaps later," she murmured. "I suddenly...uh...am not feeling at all well."

Choosing to stand in the shadows as dusk fell, she saw Celia give her a knowing glance, but stepped aside anyway as the dancers began taking their places.

When the square dance began, Faye tapped her toe, aching to join in. At the sight of Joe moving from woman to woman, laughing and joking with them as he swung them around in time with the music, she felt a surge of jealousy. She folded her arms across her chest and tried to ignore his tormenting glances, attempting in vain to focus her attention on the caller.

As the dancing continued, Joe appeared to be getting more excited, sweeping his partners off their feet at the conclusion of the "miner's delight," "set your partners," or "gents to the right."

Unable to bear any more Faye lifted the hem of her skirt and began to run into the dark shadows of the forest. She stifled a sob behind a hand, hating Joe for smiling and laughing when she was nothing but miserable.

Faye moved onward between virgin longleaf pines, the spicelike fragrance pleasantly heavy in the air. The glow of the bonfire revealed a spring-fed creek just ahead among the full-grown trees and wildflowers.

"Faye, wait up!"

Faye's insides coiled tightly when she recognized the voice. The crush of leaves meant that Joe was closing in on her. She stumbled on a fallen limb and crashed to the ground, crying out in pain when one of her hands landed on a thorny wild rose bush.

Moonlight poured through the trees overhead, silvering Faye's face as she looked up at Joe, who was suddenly standing over her, his eyes silently questioning her.

"So it's you," she said, before she even realized where the words had come from. She drew her hand from the painful thorns and rubbed the palm. "You were having a good time. What caused you to break away? If I was the cause, you have wasted your time. I don't care to dance with you. There are plenty of others eager to entertain you." She smiled devilishly up at him. "Even the wives seemed entranced by you, yet I cannot fathom why."

Joe bent over her and dug his fingers into her shoulders. Glowering down at her, he drew her up from the ground to stand before him. "I didn't come after you to ask you to dance," he said hotly. "There are more important things on my mind now that I've got you alone. Dammit, Faye, I didn't think we'd ever be alone again."

Faye winced at the pressure of his hands on her shoulders as his fingers dug more deeply into her flesh. "We've nothing else to say to each other," she said icily. "Now will you please unhand me? I was taking a stroll and do not wish to have company." She tilted her chin. "Especially not *you*."

Joe was beginning to doubt his sanity for having come after her, but he had seen too much in her eyes to quit now.

"Faye, as I saw it, you weren't taking an idle stroll," he said flatly. "You were running damned fast. What were you running away from? Your feelings for me? Or was it my apologies you were running from? Faye, I do apologize. For everything. I'm sorry I lied to you. I should have told you about Kathryn a long time ago, but I couldn't bring myself to do it. I was afraid I would lose you." He gently shook her. "Faye, do you hear me? I apologize. I want to love you now and forever. Please let me." His lips began to lower toward hers. "Please, darling? Let me?"

Faye's resistance was weakening. A sob of fury caught in her throat when his lips met hers, testing her at first with feathery kisses. Then she opened her mouth to him as he wrapped his arms fiercely around her and drew her soft pliant body into the hardness of his.

His fierce kisses dazzled her senses. Slowly her head began to reel, and the sweet pain at the juncture of her thighs was a fair warning of what could transpire if she didn't stop now.

Trying to push Joe away from her, she found that her efforts were futile. He held her pinioned in place, a prisoner of his passion and needs.

Surrendering to him, she twined her arms around his neck and returned his kiss with abandon. The rush of need within her, the heat and excitement that his kiss was arousing, suddenly alarmed her. Was she ready to forget everything just to be with him again?

But she could not fight this longing. Joe's kisses were making her forget everything. His hands molded her breasts, kneading, kindling more fires inside her. She leaned into him and felt dizzy with pleasure.

Her hands unclasped from his neck and moved down the contours of his sinewed shoulders, his straight back, and then around to touch his risen manhood through the buckskin material of his breeches. Having learned well, she moved her hands on him, knowing that what she did was right as he groaned with passion against her lips.

"Dammit," he whispered, drawing away, breathless. "What are you doing to me, woman?"

Their eyes met and held. He eased his hands from her breasts, but, wickedly, she still held her hand over him, teasing and tormenting.

"You deserve this," she said softly. "Joe, do you realize how many sleepless nights I have had since I first set eyes on you? And when I found out about that other woman? Oh, Joe, I've been in misery!"

Joe slipped her hand away and drew her savagely into his arms. Kissing her wildly, he swept her fully up into his arms and began carrying her farther into the forest, away from the music and laughter and the light of the bonfire.

"Faye, if I ever hear you mention that other woman again, I'm going to throttle you," he said huskily. "Her dress is burned now, and so is her memory. If you love me, Faye, you will accept the fact that I love only you. I want you to marry me. Soon."

"You burned the dress?" Faye gasped, her eyes wide.

"Exactly."

"You want to marry me. Soon?"

"Most definitely."

She clung to him as he still carried her determinedly away from the clearing. "But to be married, there must be a minister," she said softly. "There is only one in these parts as far as I know. And that is . . . my . . . brother."

Joe grumbled something inaudible beneath his breath as he set her down on a soft bed of grass beside the creek. "We'll just send for someone else," he said flatly. "It may take some time, but that's the way it must be done. There have been too many ill feelings between me and Michael, anyhow."

"*Oui*, I now understand that," Faye murmured, her pulse racing as Joe kissed the hollow of her throat and unsnapped her dress with his deft fingers. "I so wanted Michael to marry us. But I now know that it must be someone else."

Joe began to ease her dress and undergarments over her shoulders. "That you have agreed to marry me is a miracle," he said hoarsely. "But there won't be a miracle as far as your brother is concerned. I can understand why you are so stubborn. Like brother like sister!"

Faye laughed softly, then trembled and sucked in her breath with rapture when Joe knelt over her and flicked his tongue over her breasts, first one and then the other. She twined her fingers in his dark hair as he kissed his way down to her navel, gasping as her stomach fluttered crazily.

And when he smoothed her clothes down over her knees and gave her a fiery kiss where her need for him burned hottest, a madness seemed to engulf her.

Then he moved back up to place his brand on her lips while his hands sought and found her breasts. Her hands went to his shirt and raised it and when he eased away from her, she took it on over his head. She lay and watched as he lowered his breeches, revealing himself to her.

The cool night breeze touched Faye's naked flesh, making an involuntary shiver race up and down her spine, but this was forgotten when Joe moved over her and warmed her with the full length of his body. Her heart pounding, Faye welcomed his hardness as he probed between her thighs and then entered her swiftly and wonderfully. She lifted her legs around his waist and moved with him as his strokes within her began. His mouth seared hers with intensity as once again he kissed her, his tongue surging audaciously between her parted lips.

While crickets sang in the grass around them, Faye felt ecstasy spread within her like fine champagne, sparkling and effervescent. Her breath quickened when Joe's thrusts strengthened and his hands caressed her breasts.

She arched her body and cried out against his lips as the ultimate pleasure was reached as he plunged deeply into her.

And then a peaceful bliss settled over her as, drawing softly away from her, he looked down at her with loving eyes.

Joe wove his fingers through her hair, his eyes feasting on her slim, sinuous body in the moonlight. His heart still raced from their peak of passion, his toes still tingled from the fevered excitement.

"Darling, it's been too long," he murmured. "Let's not waste any more time in trivia. I shall send word tomorrow for a minister to come and marry us. Until then I beg of you not to let anything else antagonize you against me. Your brother will try his best, you know."

Faye traced his lips with her forefinger. "He may try, but I won't listen," she whispered, sighing when he ran his fingers down the cleavage of her breasts and then lower to slowly caress her between the thighs. "But, Joe, isn't there a way you and Michael can settle your differences? You want the same thing... law and order. Why don't you compromise?"

"As long as Father Michael believes that the vigilantes have a right in the Ozarks, then there's nothing more for me to say," Joe growled. "His mind was made up long ago. There's not a damned thing anyone can say to change his mind now. Unless..."

Faye became frantic with renewed awakenings inside her. Suddenly she feared being caught making love so wantonly out in the open. Until this moment she had been too carried away to think about it. "Joe, please don't," she said, her voice quavering as she moved his hand away from her.

Settling back, she recalled his train of thought. "Unless what?" she said, easing away from him to grab her petticoat. "What were you about to say?" She quickly slipped the petticoat over her head, glad that Joe was also dressing. He, too, must have realized the dangers of their sensual escapade.

"Unless Michael becomes the target of angry outlaws," Joe grumbled. "Then he not only places his own life in danger, but also yours and everyone else's at the mission."

"Is there really a danger?" Faye said, shivering at the thought. "And what about you? Your way of battling the outlaws surely gives them as much cause to hate you."

Joe reached for Faye and urged her to her feet. "Darling, don't worry about me," he said softly. "I can damned well take care of myself. It's you I worry about. Please watch out for any signs at the mission that might give you cause for alarm. Come for me if you feel things are becoming threatening. Will you do that?"

Faye nodded, fear creeping into her heart—a heart that only moments before felt nothing but joy. "Yes, you can depend on me."

His breath teased her ear as he drew her into his embrace. "I couldn't bear it if anything happened to you," he said thickly. "Darling, how foolish I was to fight my want of you. So many moments we could have been together are gone now forever."

"Oh, no," Faye whispered, taking a hand to guide his mouth to her lips. "My darling, we have forever to catch up, don't we?"

"Yes, forever," Joe whispered back, then claimed her lips in a fiery kiss.

Chapter Nineteen

A full day and night had passed since Faye had felt rapture in Joe's arms. If only her brother and Joe could reconcile their differences, she should not have so long to wait until their wedding vows could be exchanged.

A commotion outside in the courtyard drew Faye to the window. Slowly drawing her sheer curtains aside, she peered out into the darkness, but the moon drifting behind ragged clouds made it possible for her to see only the looming shapes of men as they dismounted from their horses and rushed into the rectory.

Dispirited and uneasy, she let the curtain fall back in place and stepped quickly away from the window. Wrapping her shawl tightly about her, she fought in vain to control a slight shiver. What she had seen most surely was uncommon. Never had men arrived at night since she had been staying at the mission.

Her hand trembling, Faye turned the doorknob, then pulled open the door and tiptoed down the long and narrow corridor to stand at the head of the staircase, listening. All that she could hear was a steady drone of voices muffled by a closed door. The visitors had gone into Michael's study, and thus far there was no sign of violence.

Still, Faye could not shake off the paralyzing dread that had seized her. She knew she must go to Joe and tell him that some sort of trouble was brewing.

Stealthily, she rushed back to her room, wishing that Gayland had not moved from the rectory and into his own house. It would have been much simpler to include him in her worries. But as it was, Gayland and Celia's cabin stood much farther from the mission than Joe's.

Hurriedly, she sorted through her clothes until she found a heavy riding skirt and long-sleeved blouse. Tonight there would not be time to hitch a horse to a buggy. Nor could she chance the noise of a clumsy buckboard wagon as it left the courtyard. If Michael were to catch her riding to Joe Harrison's cabin in the middle of the night, he would possibly lock her in her room and throw away the key.

After dressing in her riding attire, she moved stealthily from the room and down the stairs, through the kitchen and out the back door. The night was dark with the moon still hidden behind the clouds. Faint lamplight guided her to the stable where a lantern hung just inside the door.

Finding a mare that looked back at her with gentle brown eyes, Faye smoothed on a pair of riding gloves one finger at a time and smiled weakly at the horse.

Grabbing a saddle and bridle, Faye readied the horse and led her from the building. Stealthily she guided the horse along the dark edges of the mission wall, then ran with it through the gate until she felt safe enough to finally mount.

Placing a foot in the stirrup, she swung herself up and lifted the reins. As she rode deep into the darkness of the forest, she could not shake the feeling of dread that encompassed her. What if she couldn't find Joe's cabin by night? She could get lost and never be found in this region thick with saplings and scrub... a pathless maze of briars and vines. Every gust of wind through the trees brought whistles and moans.

She slapped her reins, urging the mare into a quick trot around the maze of trees only to find herself engulfed in a disorienting fog. Panic seized her heart when she no longer knew what course she had taken. Still, she drove herself on in desperation through the thick tangles of trees and brambles, a musky smell causing her nose to curl with distaste.

She could hear the pounding of her blood in her ears when she realized that the terrain had changed beneath her horse's hooves. She was being jerked around in the saddle as the horse began having trouble lifting its hooves from the sandy mud of a bog.

Faye clung tightly to the reins and tried to peer through the fog to see exactly where she had led the horse. Fear quickened her heartbeat as she recalled the tales of the swamps in these parts, a portion of low land covered partially with water, called wet meadows by some, fens by others.

The fen soil had the characteristics of loose jelly in a jar. In some places it was known that a horse could sink to its depth and disappear, in others a mass of intertwining roots formed a safety net beneath the soil.

The mare whinnied loudly and shook its mane as its right front leg became imbedded to its knee, throwing it off balance. Faye screamed as she was tossed sideways, momentarily stunned from the impact of falling to the ground that bordered the outer fringes of the swamp. The wind knocked from her lungs, it was all Faye could do to rise up on one elbow.

The mare snorted and grunted, making vain attempts to pull herself from the muck. Faye could feel its eyes on her through the darkness, pleading. The horse most surely already know its fate. More than likely its one leg had been broken by the plunge into the swamp.

Faye moved to her feet, searching through the fog with her hands, careful not to fall into the swamp herself. Finally, she reached and found the muscled shoulder of the horse, flinching at the feel of the cold and clammy perspiration on its flesh. Tears flowed down Faye's cheeks. When she smoothed her hand down the mare's leg, she knew for certain that it was broken. The bone protruded through the skin at the knee, and a sick, bitter bile rose in Faye's throat.

Finding the horse's powerful neck, Faye leaned dangerously over the swampy mass of soil and hugged the horse. "I'm so sorry," she cried. "I didn't mean for this to happen."

The horse whinnied softly in response, and Faye ran her hand over the broad forehead. "I have to leave you, you know," she murmured. "I must find my way out of here. When I do I'll send someone back for you."

She choked on a sob. She would be sending someone back to put the horse out of its misery. There was no other way.

Faye wrenched herself away from the mare. Wiping her nose with the back of a hand, she stepped away from the swampy terrain and searched with her feet for solid ground. Taking off once more through the inky, dark fog, she tried to retrace her steps, then find the path she must have missed that headed in the direction of Joe's cabin.

Breathless, nervous perspiration beading her cool brow, Faye stumbled on through the thicket of briars, unable to shake off the paralyzing fear that was building within her. She did not seem to have gotten any farther. Had she been moving in circles? Everywhere she looked, the vegetation looked the same and the damnable fog was like a white net ensnaring her with each footstep that she took.

The hair rising on the back of her neck, she listened cautiously to the sounds all around her. First there was a rush, then a rustle. Each time she found that it was only the wind.

Her knees weak and her side aching from the constant push to move onward, Faye forced one foot ahead of the other. Time seemed to have stood still. She had no idea how long she had been searching for a way out of this nightmare. Perhaps she would never emerge alive.

The sound of horses in the night caused Faye's heartbeat to quicken and a dryness to rise in her throat. She stopped and leaned an ear in the direction of the sound, recognizing that the riders were from somewhere close by.

"*A l'aide!* Help!" she screamed. "Someone. Anyone! *S'il vous plaît.* Please help me!"

Joe drew his reins tautly, causing his horse to shimmy to a sudden halt. He leaned forward in his saddle and listened, looking ahead to where fog blanketed the forest with a white mist. He gave Bart a questioning glance. "Did you hear something?" he asked guardedly. "I swear I believe I heard a woman yelling for help."

Another scream of panic reached his ears. His face paled when he recognized the voice.

"Dammit, it's Faye!" he shouted, whipping the horse with the reins, thundering on ahead with Bart following. "What in hell is she doing way out here this time of night?"

A cold sweat of fear popped up on his brow as he envisioned Faye stumbling into the swamp and drowning. He sank his heels into the flanks of his horse and rode more quickly onward, the fog now a threat to finding her.

As he traveled in a fast gallop, the fog wrapped him within its cottony arms.

Faye began to run in the direction of the thundering horses, almost limp from the damp chill and exhaustion. When the horses drew rein beside her, she looked up but could not make out the figures through the thick fog.

Then, when one of the men dismounted, and strong, familiar arms suddenly enveloped her, the voice that she had learned to love spoke gently and comfortingly to her. She broke into a soft cry and clung to Joe.

"Joe," she sobbed. "I was so afraid. I thought I might never be found."

Joe held her close, caressing her back long enough to settle her down, then spoke gently into her ear as he pressed his cheek to hers. "Why on earth are you out here?" he murmured, not wanting to scold her when she was so frightened.

"Several men came to the mission and were meeting with Michael," Faye said breathlessly. "I became frightened because I've never seen men congregate like that at night with my brother. I didn't know if they were vigilantes or outlaws. When there was no gunfire or commotion, I had to guess it was vigilantes. But they were there for a reason. I thought I had best come to warn you. Surely there is trouble brewing in the area."

"It seems that word of the outlaws' activities has spread faster than we realized, Bart," Joe said, speaking to Bart over Faye's shoulder. "The vigilantes who met at Father Michael's must be from his congregation. Most likely they were receiving his blessing before riding out to do their dirty business."

"They need more than a blessing," Bart growled, leaning on the pommel of his saddle. "They need the fear of God knocked into them!"

Joe looked into Faye's eyes. "How did you get here?" he asked softly. "Why are you on foot?"

Faye looked back over her shoulder, trying to orient herself so that she could lead Joe to the horse. "Joe, I took a mare from Michael's stable and ... and ... her hooves got stuck in the swamp," she said. She looked up at Joe. "Her leg is broken, Joe. She has to be put out of her misery."

Joe drew Faye within his embrace, again giving comfort to her.

"What's the next move, Joe?" Bart asked, having dismounted. As his gaze met Joe's, his hand rested on a holstered revolver.

"I'd best take Faye back to my cabin and get her settled in by the fire," Joe said thickly. "She appears to be chilled clear through to the bone. You go search for her horse and do what is needed, then go on to the fort. After I make sure Faye is all right, I'll come to the fort. She'll stay at my cabin until the danger has passed."

"Whatever you say," Bart said, going back to his horse and swinging himself up in the saddle. "I'll go and find Faye's horse. I have a pretty good notion where it is."

Drawing Faye up into his arms, Joe carried her to his horse and placed her in the saddle. Mounting behind her, he held her close as he began riding back in the direction of his cabin.

"Please don't call me foolish for having come, Joe," Faye said, turning to him to rest against his powerful chest. "I was so worried about Michael."

"Yes, I know," he grumbled. "But I knew he'd get you in trouble one way or another."

His eyes met hers as she looked up at him. "After tonight, Faye, never again," he said stiffly. "Tomorrow we're going to Father Michael, and he'll marry us if I have to hold a revolver to his heart to force him into it. I'm not going to leave you under his care another night. Do you understand?"

"You'll force him?" Faye gasped.

"That's only a matter of speaking," Joe replied, chuckling.

"I would hope so." Faye sighed, and relaxed against him once more.

"But he will marry us, Faye," Joe said determinedly.

When a single gunshot rang through the air, Faye flinched. She trembled and clung to Joe with all of her strength, tears flooding her eyes at the thought of the beautiful mare....

Chapter Twenty

Huddled before the fireplace in Joe's cabin, Faye shivered from the chill, even though a blanket was drawn around her shoulders. Slowly she sipped a cup of coffee.

"You'll be all right here," Joe reassured her, readjusting his gun belt on his hips. "It seems that the outlaws have chosen to go elsewhere tonight."

Faye looked up at Joe. "Will Michael be all right?" she asked, placing the cup on a table beside her. "Perhaps those men who went to see Michael will draw the outlaws to the mission. Michael and everyone there would be in danger."

Joe knelt on one knee beside Faye and wove his fingers through her tangled hair. "I'm sure Father Michael isn't in any danger tonight," he said softly. "It is the vigilantes who must watch their backs. They must have heard the news of the outlaws' plans the same as Bart. I hope the army will have the chance to hunt down and capture the outlaws first."

Joe rose and reached for the rifle laid across the antlers above the door. "Father Michael will be all right *if* the vigilantes steer clear of trouble tonight. I guess I should add," he said hoarsely, priming and loading the rifle, "if the vigilantes interfere with law and order, then Father Michael has much to fear. Though your brother does not belong directly to the vigilance committee, the outlaws surely know that he entices people to join it. That can mean only disaster for him in the end."

Faye rose shakily, her eyes wide. "I'd best return to the mission," she said. "I must go to Michael. He must be made to understands the dangers."

Weak from her ordeal, she stumbled in her efforts to cross the room. Joe placed the rifle aside and guided her to his bed. "You aren't going anywhere," he said flatly. "You're staying right here in my bed. Do you hear?"

"But, my brother could be killed," Faye protested softly.

"Darling, he understands the dangers and has turned his back to any warnings," Joe said, easing Faye down onto the bed. "You can't do anything about it. No one can. Only Father Michael can make that decision. It's between him and his God."

Even though the bed was a mat of corn husks and leaves, it felt good to her all the same, and she snuggled down into it. Her eyes closed wearily. "I'm so tired,'' she murmured, lying on her side. "Oh, Joe, tonight has thus far been so horrible!''

Drawing a patchwork quilt over Faye, Joe looked down at her for a moment, taken by her vulnerability and wanting to protect her. "Rest, darling,'' he whispered, bending to kiss her softly on the cheek. "I hope I won't be long. Remember what we have planned for tomorrow? We'll go to Michael. He'll marry us or be damned!''

Faye wanted to feel radiantly happy over Joe's determination to marry her so quickly, but she knew that Michael would never agree to it. If only life were as simple as Joe tried to make it.

Turning to face Joe, Faye twined her arms around his neck and kissed him hungrily. "Joe, please be careful,'' she pleaded softly. "Come back to me unharmed.''

Joe cupped her face between his hands and kissed the tip of her nose. "Go to sleep, darling,'' he whispered. "When you awaken, I will have already taken care of business and returned home.''

Her eyes still closed, Faye nodded, feeling the lethargic wonders of sleep already claiming her. She sighed deeply, unaware of Joe placing a loaded rifle on the bed beside her for protection in case all that he had predicted did not come to pass.

Quietly, Joe stepped away from Faye and slapped the revolvers at his hips as he rushed toward the door.

He hoped he wasn't too late to join the cavalry. Bart was sure to have caught up with them by now.

Chasing outlaws had gotten in his blood. The danger of it made his heart pound with excitement.

Hurrying outside, he placed a foot in the stirrup and swung himself up into his saddle and flicked his horse's reins. Galloping through the darkness, he nodded a thank-you to the clouds as they slipped away, leaving the moon clear and full. The narrow road was now well lit, and everything was so peaceful and beautiful that it was hard to believe that anything could be wrong. The only sounds he heard were the occasional hooting of an owl and the rush of the Arkansas River.

Suddenly Joe's insides coiled tightly. The very identifiable sound of approaching horses from behind him made his heart skip a beat. Bart could not have reached the fort this quickly and returned with the cavalry. That had to mean that the approaching horsemen were a part of the outlaw gang.

Joe looked up at the moon, now cursing it. As soon as the outlaws caught sight of him, they would know who he was. He was too well-known by them not to be recognized.

Bending low over the flying mane of his horse, Joe thrust his heels into its flanks and flicked the reins, but the outlaws were gaining on him much too quickly. They must have been waiting for him on the road, waiting for the right moment to chase him down.

At least the outlaws had not tried to capture him in his cabin, riddling it with bullets before setting it on fire. Faye was most surely safe enough in his absence.

The thundering of hooves behind him made Joe realize that he could no longer outrun them. They were now only a stone's throw away. As a bullet whizzed over his head, he knew that he had no choice but to make a daring escape.

If he survived, he would be lucky.

Joe left the road and rode into the forest, rushing past pine and hickory trees and deep ravines. His heart thundering, Joe sucked in his breath as he approached the sheer bluff. Exhaling heavily, he led the horse on over the bluff, extricating himself from the saddle so that he and the horse would land separately in the water.

The few seconds it took to fall seemed like an eternity. He struggled to straighten his body as the night air rushed over him, then managed to land feet first in the water safely enough away from the jutting rocks lining the banks.

Plummeting down into the dark abyss of the river, Joe fought dizziness and the pain racking his lungs as he clung desperately to consciousness. When he bobbed back up to the surface, gasping, he wiped his hair back from his eyes and searched around him for his horse. He felt nauseated when he saw that his horse had not been as lucky. Its broken and bleeding body lay on a ledge way beyond Joe's reach.

Treading water, Joe stared blankly at the horse that had been so dependable and trusting all these years. He would never find another horse as likable...as gentle... Looking at the tragic scene, he cursed the outlaws.

At the thought, he gazed up at the bluff and saw the silhouette of the horsemen as they peered down at the river. Joe was glad that his hair was dark and that his face was bronze; at such distance, he would be undetectable.

Having regained his breath, Joe dived beneath the water and swam hurriedly to the other shore.

Grasping the thick tufts of grass that grew along the bank, Joe pulled himself out of the water. Winded and wet, chilled to the bone, he flopped down on his back, breathing hard. He closed his eyes and rested for a moment, then a low nickering from somewhere close by drew them wildly open again.

His hand quickly withdrew a revolver from its holster as he crept to his knees and looked cautiously from side to side. The horse, and possibly a rider, had to be close by.

His heart thudding hard within his chest, he moved deftly to his feet and eased behind some bushes, no longer hearing any sounds and not seeing any horse. The moonlight at his feet guided his eyes downward. Then he dropped to his knees and studied the riverbank rimmed with hoofprints.

Suddenly a twig snapped and hoofbeats sounded on soft earth behind him. Joe glanced cautiously back over his shoulder. Almost within touching distance, the bulky undefined shapes of horses now loomed behind him as they moved toward the river. He lowered his pistol to his side when he discovered that they were all without riders.

Joe shivered in his wet clothes as he began inching his way downwind along the bank, and then smiled smugly to himself when he found the fence that had been built to the edge of the river.

Idly, he scratched his brow. It looked as though the outlaws had built a nice corral for their stolen horses. Most likely they would be increasing the numbers within the next few hours if they were successful in their raids.

A few seconds passed before he moved back toward the horses. The one closest to him blew out a snort and then began drinking, still oblivious of being watched. Then Joe's head jerked around and he tried to quiet his breathing as he heard someone idly whistling a tune from somewhere close by.

Joe studied his wet weapon, now unsure of its accuracy, but a man feeling its barrel stuck in his ribs would not know the difference.

Stooping, he moved stealthily through the low-hanging limbs of cottonwoods and oaks. Then, squinting, he began looking for the outlaw. It wasn't long before he spied him sitting casually beneath a tree, smoking a cigar and taking occasional drinks from a whiskey bottle. Joe smiled to himself.

Making sure his moccasinned feet did not make a sound, Joe circled around to approach the outlaw from behind. As the man took another long swallow of whiskey, Joe lunged forward and with the butt of his revolver rendered the outlaw unconscious with a fierce blow to the head.

As the outlaw slouched over, Joe stepped around in front of him, breathing hard. Twirling the revolver back into his holster, he knelt and disarmed the man, thrusting the outlaw's revolver into the waist of his own breeches.

His gaze moved quickly around him, finding the outlaw's horse still saddled and grazing nearby. His eyes locked on the rifle resting in its leather sheath at the side of the horse, then shifted to the rope looped around the pommel of the saddle.

With long, quick steps, Joe went and grabbed the rope and tied the outlaw's hands behind him. Grunting, he lifted the man and carried him to the horse and swung him over the rear and tied him in place, then mounted and headed toward the trail leading back to Fort Smith. Once he delivered the outlaw to the fort, he could then lead the soldiers back to the corralled horses. After they were rounded up and taken back to Fort Smith, the settlers would have a grand time choosing theirs out of the many.

Joe's thoughts were diverted when he heard approaching horses heading toward the corral. He drew his revolver and pulled his mount to a sudden halt, sidling the horse behind a thick stand of cottonwoods.

A sigh escaped him when he recognized Bart as one of the lead riders. He spurred his horse out into the open and reined in beside his fellow scout.

"Good God, man," Bart said, craning his neck to see who was secured to the horse Joe now made claim to. "Who is that?" His gaze swept over the horse. "Joe, where's your own horse?"

Joe set his jaw firmly and glanced over his shoulder at the outlaw just stirring from unconsciousness. "It's a long story," he growled. "But I'm glad you happened along. There are a few horses up the way needing to be returned to owners."

"How are things going for you?" he asked Bart dryly. "But I don't have to guess. It's obvious you have no outlaws in tow."

Bart laughed throatily and leaned closer to Joe. "Now I wouldn't say that," he said smoothly. "We rounded up some just a few miles down the road. They're being escorted to the guardhouse at the fort all unarmed and tied up. Strangest damned thing—they came riding down the middle of the road just like they owned the thing."

Joe smiled smugly. "I think I know which outlaws you're speaking of," he said, chuckling. "I'm damned glad you caught them. I'm minus a horse because of 'em."

He raked his fingers through his wet hair nervously. "I came near to also losing my life," he said thickly.

Bart looked Joe up and down. "Joe, it looks like you have had some night," he said, frowning. "Let me take the son of a bitch outlaw off your hands, and you return home and get outta those wet clothes. Just lead us to the horses and we can take care of the rest."

Troubled by Faye's being all alone in the cabin, Joe nodded. "Yes, I think I'll do just that," he said tensely. With that, he swung his horse around and began riding in the opposite direction. "Follow me. The horses aren't far."

The small posse followed him, their horses' hooves sounding like distant thunder in the still of the night.

Chapter Twenty-one

Absorbing the warmth of the fire into his damp, cold flesh, Joe tossed his wet shirt aside and stepped out of his clinging buckskin breeches. By the flickering light of the fire, he ran a towel briskly over his muscled body, then turned and looked at Faye stirring slightly on his bed.

Letting the towel drop to the floor, he studied her as the glow from the fire illuminated her face. When her eyes slowly opened, as though she was aware of being watched, he smiled down at her.

Faye blinked nervously, then rubbed her eyes with the backs of her hands. The outline of Joe's naked body was silhouetted against the fire.

"Faye?" Joe said, moving toward her. "How are you feeling?"

Shaken by the sudden presence of his nude form, she watched nervously as he settled himself under the covers beside her, drawing the patchwork quilt over him. "*Oui*, I'm feeling fine," she said in a rush.

She trembled as he fitted his body into the curve of hers and turned her to face him. Placing a hand to his brow, she smoothed a lock of hair back in place, "Did you leave me here, darling, only to seduce me upon your return?" she questioned softly.

Then her brow puckered in a worried frown as she raised up on one elbow. "Oh, Joe, you are here," she cried softly. "What happened to you?"

"Shh," he reassured softly. "Everything is all right. Don't worry about a thing." He gave her a fleeting kiss on her lips. "Everything is all right except for my heart. Being with you like this is making it beat double hard."

He cuddled her closer. "What can you do about that?" he asked, nuzzling her neck, his fingers deftly unbuttoning her blouse.

Faye's breath was stolen as he pulled her blouse open and bent his head to flick his tongue around a nipple. She twined her arms around his neck and ran her fingers down the taut muscles of his back, the sleek hardness of his shoulders and flat belly, and then his pulsing manhood. Circling her fingers around him, she thrilled to his sudden intake of breath.

"Darling, not yet," Joe said huskily, brushing her hand aside. He tossed the patchwork quilt away and began lowering her skirt and then her petticoat.

Sensuously, he moved slowly over her, positioning himself above her nude body. His lips beckoned hers to yield to him as he captured her mouth in a fierce, fevered kiss.

His hands moved over her body, touching her with hungry need. Softly, she moaned against his insistent lips, stiffening as he made a wild plunge. Then he began to move within her with exquisite tenderness, all the while running his fingers down her body, caressing her, intoxicating her.

She strained upward to meet his thrusts, abandoning herself to the wondrous feelings that were encompassing her. She could feel her excitement rising. She clung to him. She moaned.

Joe stifled her sweet declaration of pleasure with another fiery kiss. At the feel of the satin texture of her flesh, the throbbing of her heart against the palm of his hand, the stiff peaks of her breasts, the burning in his loins raging higher and higher.

Withdrawing from her, he raised up and knelt on either side of her, looking down at her adoringly. His eyes lit with fire as he swept them over her gentle curves. His blood quickened with passion as she looked back up at him, so innocent, yet so wantonly a woman needing to be pleasured!

"I do love you so much," Joe said, his hands caressing her breasts. "Let me show you just how much, darling."

Her eyes hazed over with passion, she watched as he began loving her with his mouth and tongue, beginning at the hollow of her throat, working his way down. Even when he kissed the bottoms of her feet and ran his tongue over the soles she felt pleasure.

But when he began working his way up again, leaving a flaming path of rapture in his wake, she could bear no more. "Joe, please?" she murmured, placing her hands to his shoulders, easing him up again so that their lips could meet in a tender kiss. "I can hardly wait any longer. Make love to me now. Please."

Joe sealed her lips with a fiery kiss as he dived into her once again and began his rhythmic strokes. His fingers dug into her buttocks and drew her more tightly against him. He worked frantically, sensing the peak nearing....

Faye was feeling the incredible sweetness blossoming within her. And then she could hold back no longer. Her whole body quivered as a mindless bliss claimed her. She clung and rocked with Joe as his body seemed to explode while he held her ever so close. Their bodies fused together, experiencing the same marvelous sensations as though they were one.

And then it was over.

Their bodies damp with perspiration, they lay snuggled close, breathing hard. Faye smoothed Joe's hair back from his brow and became breathless when he kissed first one breast and then the other before drawing her close once more.

"I never want to let you go," Joe whispered, his fingers at the nape of her neck urging her lips to his. "Kiss me again, darling."

A sound of gunfire and the shattering of glass made Joe and Faye pull apart. They exchanged quick, troubled glances as they both saw the broken window on the other side of the room. Joe grabbed Faye and forced her back down on the bed and covered her with his own body as bullets riddled the windows and walls.

"Dammit!" Joe said in a choking tone.

He grabbed Faye and bodily shoved her beneath the bed, tossing a blanket to her. "Stay there until I say it's all right to come out!"

Shivering with fear as she clutched the blanket around her, Faye looked wildly at Joe. Calmly, he sat down on the floor beside the bed and worked himself into his breeches. "Joe, what's happening?" she cried. "Who is doing the shooting?"

"Only one guess," Joe growled, finally fastening the breeches in place. "It's a band of outlaws that didn't get captured tonight. They've come to make sure they kill me this time."

"What do you mean . . . this time?" Faye gasped.

"They tried already once tonight, that's what," he said, crawling on his belly to grab the rifle that lay close by. "This time they just might succeed."

"Oh, Joe, please be careful," Faye cried, fear gripping her. "You surely don't have a chance!"

"Not a chance in hell as I see it," he rasped beneath his breath so that she could not hear.

He flinched as another volley of bullets bounced off the wall just above his head. The outlaws shouted and laughed loudly as they continued firing. Suddenly the shooting ceased. In the brief silence, Joe made out the sound of approaching horses. Joe held his breath, waiting.

A second later, gunfire erupted again. This time the guns were aimed in a different direction. Joe said a quiet prayer of thanks and inched his way over to the window.

In the flood of moonlight he could see outlaws fleeing on foot into the forest. Bart was riding among the fleeing outlaws, kicking them with the heel of his moccasin and knocking others in the head with the butt of his rifle.

The soldiers were scattering their horses along the land preventing the outlaws from reaching their horses tethered in the forest nearby. Some gave chase, some fired at the outlaws, and others jumped from their horses to wrestle them to the ground.

Joe opened the cabin door, only to find one of the marauders intent on entering. With instinctive reflexes, Joe took aim and fired point-blank into the chest of the outlaw. In a matter of moments he would have been inside the cabin.

"Hang in there, Joe!" Bart shouted, laughing. He swung himself out of the saddle and went and stood beside Joe, taking shots at those outlaws who had yet to make it to the protection of the forest.

Then the gunfire finally ceased. Joe blew smoke from his rifle and stood square-shouldered as he looked at the death and destruction that interrupted his night with Faye.

He went to the outlaw who had almost succeeded in getting inside the cabin. Venomously, Joe glared down at the sightless eyes. "You bastard," Joe grumbled. "You'll never steal again—or take shots at me and my woman!"

"Your woman?" Bart gasped, looking toward the cabin. "Faye?"

Having heard the silence Faye had crawled from beneath the bed and had slipped hurriedly into her blouse and skirt. Trembling, she crept toward the door and eased it open, then ran to Joe when she saw him standing there unharmed.

"Darling, darling…" she said, clinging to him, her eyes wide as she looked around her and saw the bloody remains of the outlaws. She shuddered intensely and turned her eyes away.

"Yes, I see she's all right," Bart said, smiling from Faye to Joe.

"Come on inside," Joe said to Faye, holding her face close to his chest so that she could not see any more of the bloody scene.

Joe led Faye back into his cabin, stepping over broken glass and chunks of wood. Joe gave Bart a hard glance as he followed. "What brought you and the soldiers here?"

"We didn't get the horses rounded up," Bart said, apology in his tone. "Just as we started to, some of the outlaws returned. We had quite a battle on our hands, but we arrested some of 'em. I suspected that the ones that got away are the same ones who paid you this little social call. They know that you and I work as partners, so they surely decided it was just as well to shoot you as me. That's when I decided it was best to follow and check on you."

"Well, we still have some of them to worry about, don't we?" Joe growled, easing Faye down onto a chair before the simmering fire. He grabbed a blanket and placed it around her shoulders. "I wonder what their next move will be?"

"I think things'll be quiet for the rest of the night, Joe," Bart said, nodding. He gave Faye a gentle glance. "I'll leave you to your woman, but I'm posting a couple of soldiers outside just in case."

"That sounds fine to me," Joe said, looking all around, seeing exactly what the outlaws could do in no time flat. "Who's to say what they *will* do next?"

Faye looked up at Joe and swallowed hard. "Do you think Michael is in danger?" she said, her voice strained. "What if...?"

Joe leaned down and placed a finger to her lips. "Now let's not borrow trouble," he said thickly. "I don't think the outlaws are going to try anything else tonight."

Bart looked uneasily over at Joe. "I'm not so sure about that," he said blandly. "The vigilantes stirred up a peck of trouble tonight. They were positioned inside a few settlers' houses waiting for the first signs of trouble. They got a few shots at some outlaws. One outlaw, the one called Winthrop, even got captured and is now swinging from a tree, his neck broke. So I do suspect the outlaws will be out for blood . . . a vigilante's blood."

Faye clasped her fingers fiercely to Joe's arm. "I've got to go to Michael," she gasped.

Joe took her wrists and held her close to him. "Now you listen to me," he said determinedly. "You're not going anywhere. You heard Bart. There will be soldiers posted here tonight. I want you here where I know you'll be safe."

"But my brother isn't!"

"That's his problem."

Faye tried to wrench herself free. "Joe, let me go," she cried. "I can't just sit here and wait for my brother to be killed!"

Joe gave Bart a heavy look. "Will you see to it that a couple of soldiers are positioned close to the mission, also?" he asked, his jaw tight. "I don't want Faye worrying."

Bart squinted hard as he studied Joe's expression. Then he looked at Faye and saw how worried she was. "Yeah, I'll see to it," he said, ambling toward the door. "I'll leave you two alone. I think you can rest peacefully enough now." He winked over his shoulder at Joe. "Good ol' Bart came through for you, huh?"

Joe smiled at him. "As always," he said, giving Bart a mock salute as he moved on from the cabin, closing the door behind him.

He drew Faye up from the chair and into his arms, and they stood before the fire, staring into it. "Things will be all right," he reassured her. "Tomorrow we will take a ride together to the mission. There we will be married. Then I plan to live with you happily ever after, outlaws and vigilantes be damned!"

Faye snuggled into his embrace and looked up at him adoringly. *"Merci,"* she murmured.

"Thank you for what?"

"For giving orders for soldiers to guard the mission."

"I did it for you. Not Michael."

"I know," she whispered, placing her cheek against his chest. "I know."

Chapter Twenty-two

The fire in the fireplace had burned down to dying embers, glowing orange in the night. As she snuggled beside Joe, Faye's sleep was disturbed by a nightmare. She moaned and jerked away from Joe, gunfire exploding all around her in her dream.

And then in her dream an outlaw turned his pistol to Michael, took aim and...

Wrenched awake, Faye sat upright and began screaming. Joe jumped with a start. Drawing her into his arms, he gently rocked her.

In Faye's mind's eye she was still seeing the outlaw aiming at Michael. In another split second she would have seen the ball pierce her brother's black robe and then his flesh! It had seemed so real...

She clutched Joe, reveling in the feel of his warm flesh against hers. "Joe, it was so horrible," she cried, shivering. "I was dreaming of outlaws. First they were shooting at me, and then...and then...just before I awoke, one outlaw had turned to Michael and was ready to shoot him.''

Pulling back from Joe, she implored him with her tear-filled eyes, panic rising within her. "Joe, I've got to go to Michael," she blurted. "The nightmare could be a warning. Perhaps it could be warning me of what is to happen to Michael."

She moved quickly from the bed and searched through the semidarkness for her clothes. "I must return to the mission," she said, her voice quavering.

Joe was struck dumb by her reaction to the dream. He looked toward the windows. The moon was still bright; it was still the middle of the night.

Bolting to his feet, he went to Faye and stopped her as she reached for her discarded clothes. "You're being foolish," he growled. "Do you know what time it is? What's Father Michael going to think about your morals when you enter the rectory at this ungodly hour? Tomorrow we plan to convince your brother one way or the other to marry us. It's best that we arrive tomorrow, and to hell with what he thinks about us spending a full night together. We will be man and wife within the hour."

"But the nightmare?" Faye said, again shivering. "It has to have meant something."

"If everybody paid attention to all their nightmares, the world would be full of fanatics," Joe said softly. He eased an arm around her bare waist and began leading her back to the bed. "Now, come on. Let's try to get a few more winks of sleep, and when morning comes we'll head out bright and early to go to the mission."

The strange, foreboding uneasiness refused to go away. Not to be easily dissuaded, Faye placed a determined hand to Joe's arm and brushed it away from her.

"No matter what you say, I must return to the mission tonight," she said resolutely. She stooped down then and picked up her clothes. "Whether or not Michael catches me entering the rectory in the middle of the night, I must go and see if he is all right."

Joe braced his hands on his hips and glowered down at Faye as she pulled her dress over her head. "And where does that leave me?" he asked. "Don't you know that if I leave you there tonight, we may never have a life together. If your brother has checked your room and found you gone, there's no way in hell he will marry us."

"My bother has always respected my privacy," Faye said dryly. "Once I have retired to my bedroom for the night, he never interferes with my privacy. Right now he most surely believes that I am fast asleep only a few doors down from his own bedroom. Unless..."

She shivered at the thought of the outlaws having possibly gone to the rectory to seek revenge. "Unless he isn't in his room, either," she said, her voice breaking.

Seeing that her stubborn streak was not to be broken, Joe tightened his jaw. If he didn't escort her to the mission, he knew damned well that she would take off all alone and go there by herself.

"I think you'll regret this," he said, jerking on his buckskin trousers. "This could affect our whole future. But if you feel that you must do this, I won't stand in your way."

"*Oui*, I must," Faye said, clasping her hands tightly together behind her as she waited by the door for Joe to finish dressing. Her gaze lowered and she gasped when she saw the wrinkles on her skirt and blouse. She uttered a silent prayer that when she arrived at the mission everyone *would* be fast asleep.

Looking at Faye dressed in only her blouse and skirt, Joe yanked a blanket from the bed and wrapped it around her shoulders. "This should keep you warm enough," he said, searching her face as the embers of the fire cast their orange shadows upon her. "I love you, Faye. I can't lose you. No matter what, I can't lose you."

Faye looked up at his handsomeness and swallowed hard. She was waiting for him to embrace her, but instead he went to a chair and grabbed his gun belt and buckled it around his waist, placed a sheathed knife close to one of his revolvers, then swung the door open wide.

Faye followed Joe outside into the path of the moonlight. And then she welcomed his powerful arms as he placed her on the horse in front of him and rode toward the mission, holding her close to him.

Faye clasped the blanket tightly as it whipped around her. With every muscle in her body, she struggled to stay atop the horse, close to Joe as he spurred the horse to a full gallop.

Suddenly a muffled scream tore through the darkness. Faye lurched and grabbed Joe's arm in fright. Joe jumped with alarm and reined in the horse to a slow trot.

"Joe, someone is in pain," Faye said, goose bumps rising along her flesh as another scream ripped through the silence of the night. "I've heard the cry of mountain lions since I've been in Arkansas, but that wasn't a mountain lion. That was the scream of a woman."

Joe's dark eyes scanned the trees, looking for signs of life. "It's a woman, all right," he growled. "But where is she?"

The horse sauntered on along the winding path as Faye and Joe kept searching the dark forest. When the woman screamed again, the sound was so close that Faye knew for sure they would find her.

"Over there!" Joe said, drawing the horse to a halt. He quickly dismounted and held his arms up to Faye and helped her down.

Frightened, Faye followed behind him as he elbowed his way through the thick vegetation.

"My God," Joe said, his voice sounding strangled as he suddenly fell on his knees to the ground. There lay an Osage squaw swollen with child, her sweat-covered face etched with pain and her loosely fitted cotton dress soiled and ripped.

Faye's footsteps faltered as she moved to Joe's side and stared down at the pitiful sight. She shuddered intensely and covered her mouth at the sight of the blood-stained ground beneath the woman.

Then she forced down the bitter bile rising in her throat as the woman looked up at her with dark, pain-filled eyes and reached out for her with her hands.

"Help...me..." the woman pleaded softly. "My baby. My baby is ready to be born. I feel... so...weak. Please help me. Save my baby."

Joe and Faye exchanged quick, uneasy glances then looked back down at the woman as she grabbed at her abdomen and screamed again. Closing her eyes to hide the tears, she panted loudly in an attempt to catch her breath.

Faye moved to her knees beside the woman and took one of her hands. "We're here to help you," she said reassuringly. "Don't worry. The baby will be all right. We'll see to that."

She looked over at Joe who was studying her silently. She smiled at him and blushed, for she surely knew his thoughts. He would not expect her to be able to help a woman in childbirth. But she must, not only to help the woman, but to help an innocent child.

"Are you sure?" Joe asked, removing his knife from its leather sheath. "It will be quite unpleasant, Faye."

"I imagine so," she murmured. "In the end it will be worth it, won't it? We will have helped this woman bring her child into the world."

The woman opened her eyes and smiled from Faye to Joe. "My name is Nightwind. Nightwind is glad you have come," she whispered, breathing harshly. "When the child arrives, it will not die on the ground. It will live in your arms."

Faye shivered violently, then once again composed herself. "No," she murmured. "The child won't die on the ground."

Nightwind closed her eyes and bit her lower lip as another pain tore through her. She clutched Faye's hand, squeezing hard, then once again relaxed when the contraction was gone. "Soon," Nightwind whispered. "Soon."

Faye nodded, then looked at the pool of blood on the ground. She silently questioned Joe with her eyes.

He shook his head, telling her without words that the woman was hemorrhaging and that she would more than likely not last through the birth.

"Winthrop sent me from his house when he knew it was time for me to give birth to our child," Nightwind sobbed, tears rolling down her cheeks. "First he steals me from my people and forces me to be his wife, and then discards me because I am heavy with child!"

She looked sorrowfully up at Faye. "I returned to my people, but they banished me from the village," she cried. "I've been left to wander alone for days. I'm weak from hunger. I was trying to make it to Father Michael's mission. But I started bleeding!"

Faye's expression was drawn from lines of sadness, and again she had to force down bitter bile. "I'm so sorry," she said softly. "My brother would have helped you in your time of need. You and your child would have both been all right."

"Your brother?" Nightwind asked, studying Faye closely.

"My brother is Father Michael," Faye said proudly. She leaned closer to Nightwind's face. "You said Winthrop sent you away."

At Nightwind's slight nod, Faye looked toward Joe. "Winthrop is the father of this child," she murmured. "He's the one who ran Nightwind off."

"Yeah," he rasped. "He was one of the meanest outlaws in the area. I'd have expected him to be this callous. But he won't get the chance to do this again, will he?''

Nightwind looked quickly up at Joe. "Winthrop is dead?" she said anxiously. "Is he?"

"Very," Joe said, chuckling lowly.

Nightwind closed her eyes peacefully. "That is good," she whispered. "He was an evil, cold-hearted man." She suddenly grabbed her abdomen again, her eyes wild. "It's happening!" she screamed. "The baby! It's coming."

With one quick look at each other, Faye and Joe moved quickly. Joe placed his knife at the hem of the Indian's dress and tore away the skirt. With that, Faye grabbed the material and ran to the creek that was only a few footsteps away and soaked it in the clear spring water.

When she returned, she found Nightwind's legs spread wide and Joe kneeling between them, grunting as he attempted to ease the child from her body.

Faye knelt down beside Nightwind and began wiping her brow with the cool, wet material. The squaw screamed and screamed, her eyes glazed with pain as she tossed her head wildly from side to side.

"Damn, I don't like the looks of this," Joe grumbled, still trying to free the child. "There's too much blood."

"Oh, Joe," Faye cried softly. "You must do what you can. They must live."

Their eyes met, and she wanted to break into fitful tears when he again shook his head. He then focused his full attention on the child. With a heave and sigh, he finally succeeded in extricating the child from the mother.

Faye watched anxiously as he cut the umbilical cord, then gave the baby several soft slaps. When the infant began to cry fitfully, Faye's face blossomed into a thankful smile.

Suddenly Nightwind grabbed her desperately, clawing at her skirt. Then her hands fell limply away. Faye tensed.

"No!" she gasped, looking down at eyes that were staring blankly ahead. "Nightwind, please don't die!"

Joe held the baby in his arms and went to Faye to kneel beside her. "Darling, she's already dead," he said solemnly. "Like I said, there was too much blood loss. No one could live through that. And she was weakened by having not eaten, perhaps for days. She didn't have a chance in hell of surviving this birth."

He looked down at the baby nuzzling against his buckskin shirt. "But we saved the child," he said hoarsely. "I'd say that's some sort of miracle, wouldn't you?"

Faye gazed at the child. She could tell in the moonlight that the only thing that looked Indian about the child was its thick thatch of black hair and perhaps its eyes. But the skin was as white as alabaster. "Oh, Joe, it's a sweet little girl," she murmured.

"A girl that needs to be wrapped with a blanket," Joe said, rising to his feet. His gaze moved quickly around him. "That blanket you had around you. Where is it?"

"I dropped it back by the horse," Faye said anxiously. "I'll go and get it."

She looked down at Nightwind. "What of Nightwind?" she asked, her voice breaking.

"As soon as we get the child bundled up, I'll bury her," Joe said evenly. "Then we'll take the child on into the mission. I'm sure some family will take pity on the poor thing and take her in to raise as their own."

"Yes, I'm sure," Faye said, moving hurriedly toward the horse, searching for the blanket. She stopped in midstep when she thought of Celia and Gayland. They were childless, but not because they had opted not to have children. They had tried many times. This child could be theirs to raise.

Smiling at the thought, Faye grabbed the blanket up from the ground and took it to Joe. She smiled down at the child as he wrapped the blanket around it, then she accepted the small bundle into her arms. One thing for sure, the entrance back to the mission was no longer going to be a quiet, secret one. Upon arrival she would have to awaken Michael and tell him what had happened. Somehow arrangements would have to be made to find a wet nurse.

Perhaps the child's presence would ease Faye's own return to the mission. She looked to the heavens and prayed that she was right.

Chapter Twenty-three

Joe held Faye in place in front of him with a muscled arm. The baby was wrapped securely in a blanket, and she held it tightly to her chest. He had reined in his horse to a soft trot so that the baby would not be jostled. Looking at the tiny infant's pale face, he was glad that the mission was not far ahead.

He glanced down at Faye as she clung to the child, seeing the woman he loved as nothing less than wonderful. Tonight she had proved so much to him. She was strong and capable. Surely she could survive the challenges of the wilderness.

Smiling contentedly, Joe lifted his eyes away from her, knowing that their future together was most definite. In a few hours' time they would be married.

Joe's insides tightened when through a break in the trees a bright orange glow in the sky ahead drew his attention. Without a doubt, a fire awaited them at the mission. It could only be the large church or the rectory that was on fire. The fire was much too big for a small cabin. He looked down at Faye, cursing himself for not believing in her premonition.

He realized suddenly that Faye had not noticed that anything was wrong, and Joe did not want to worry her just yet. She was too content at this moment with the child sleeping peacefully in her arms.

Knowing that he must get to the mission quickly to lend a helping hand, Joe held more tightly to Faye, flicked the reins, and thrust his moccasinned heels into the flanks of the horse, sending it into a gallop.

Faye had felt Joe's grip tighten on her just prior to his urging his horse more quickly down the path in the forest. She looked up at him with a silent questioning, finding it more and more difficult to hang on to the child and remain astride the horse.

"Joe, I feel as though I might slip!" she cried, trying to grip the saddle more firmly with her knees. "Please slow down!"

Faye looked over her shoulder as the low limbs narrowly missed hitting her in the face. Then her eyes were drawn to the sky. Everything within her grew numb at the sight of the raging fire. Her heart seemed to plummet to her feet. The church and the rectory! Just as she had feared, the outlaws had paid their visit to Michael.

"Joe, you've seen the fire also! That's why you're hurrying!" Faye cried, her hair whipping into her face. "Oh, Joe, what of Michael?"

"I'm sure he'll be all right," Joe tried to reassure her, yet he didn't believe his words for a moment.

The outlaws had done their damnedest to make their mark everywhere on this dark night. Joe had escaped their wrath twice. It seemed that Father Michael was not so lucky.

The closer the horse drew to the mission, the more prominent the aroma of smoke. Shouts and cries filled the air as the mission walls came into sight. Raging flames and thick black smoke shot up into the sky.

Faye clung to the child, her eyes wide as Joe led his horse through the gate. She gasped as she watched flames engulfing the church tower, the flames bright against the dark sky. The courtyard was a frenzy of men, women and children carrying buckets of water from the well at the back of the rectory and throwing the water onto the flames.

"It's the church!" she cried. Her gaze moved to the rectory and saw that it still stood unharmed. Hope rose that Michael was all right.

With a sick feeling in the pit of her stomach, she realized that it was during this predawn hour that Michael usually said his morning prayers at the altar before anyone else was there to interrupt his moment with God.

Joe drew his reins tight and stopped the horse. Dismounting, he reached up and lifted Faye to the ground, then turned and looked at the raging fire. It seemed that everyone was doing his part to try to save the church, but it was evident to Joe that nothing could be done. The tower now fully aflame, it would not be long until the rest of the church caught fire.

Faye looked desperately around her. A cry of panic filled her throat. "I must find out about Michael!" she exclaimed. She looked anxiously up at Joe. "Joe, see if he's all right."

Then tears filled her eyes as Celia came toward her with open arms, Gayland close behind.

"Oh, Faye, it's so terrible," Celia blurted. "We saw the flames from as far away as our cabin. We came immediately!"

Celia's footsteps faltered when she saw the bundle in Faye's arms. She opened her mouth to question Faye about the child, but Gayland interrupted her train of thought.

"Joe! It was the outlaws! They set fire to the church!" Gayland shouted, grabbing hold of Joe's arm. "Father Michael is still in the church! Several attempts have been made to rescue him, but the heat is too intense!"

A sudden dizziness swept through Faye. She teetered for a moment, then welcomed Celia's comforting arms around her to steady her. In her nightmare her brother's life had been threatened by a gun...not fire...

"I need the blanket that's wrapped around the baby," Joe said, his voice flat. He pulled off his shirt and handed it to Faye in place of the blanket. "Wrap the child in this."

Faye did as he asked, breathless with fear as she now understood what Joe was planning to do. She didn't have time to protest as he took off in a dead run toward the burning building, shouting for water to be brought to him. She watched, horrified, as he dunked the blanket into the water, then spread it around his head and shoulders and went on to the church.

When Faye saw Joe disappear into the fiery inferno, she felt as though a part of her were dying. Looking over at Celia, then down at the baby now wrapped securely in Joe's buckskin shirt, then up at Celia again, she suddenly thrust the child into Celia's arms.

Celia questioned Faye with wide, green eyes. "Whose child is this?" she said, her voice weak.

"Celia, an Indian woman gave birth to this baby a short while ago," Faye said in a rush of words. "The woman died. The child needs a home!"

Without waiting for a response, Faye began to run toward the church.

"Joe!" she cried, waving her arms frantically, starting to run into the church after him. But Gayland's strong arms grabbed her, holding her in place.

"Don't be a fool!" Gayland shouted over the roar of the flames. "Faye, your brother would not want this! You'd never make it out alive."

Faye struggled for a moment, then gave in to Gayland and stood beside him only a few feet from the church where the heat of the fire on her face was almost too hot to stand. Doubling her fists to her sides, tears streaming down her face, she watched for what seemed an eternity, and still neither Joe nor Michael came into sight. She bit her lower lip, now fearing that she might lose the two men she loved most in the world.

Then, holding her chin high, she wiped the tears away, too stubborn to believe that life could be that cruel to her. Joe would be all right. Michael would be all right. God would make it so!

Joe moved cautiously through the church, coughing and fighting the urge to flee back to the open air. Keeping the wet blanket over his head and shoulders, he tried to peer through the thick smoke to see where he was going. Feeling for the heavy wooden pews, he made his way slowly down the long aisle. Then he was able to make out the form of the elaborate altar just a few feet in front of him. Although the tower directly behind the large marble structure was engulfed in flame and the beams overhead were quietly catching fire, the altar had so far remained intact.

His footsteps quickened when he caught sight of a figure lying on the floor just ahead, a huge red velvet tapestry draped over his shoulders and face. Joe recognized Father Michael's black robe, and he was glad when he heard Michael cough and saw him attempt to get to his knees, realizing that the priest was at least conscious.

"Father Michael!" Joe said. In his exuberance, Joe sucked in too much smoke when he opened his mouth, causing his lungs to feel as though they were on fire. He coughed and wheezed. "Don't move. Wait until I reach you. I'll help you out of the church to safety!"

Michael raised his head and squinted his watering eyes. Reaching out his hand, he grabbed on to Joe's arm. "Joe!" he gasped. "Thank the Lord!"

Flinching as a beam fell from the ceiling and crashed in flames beside the altar, Joe grabbed the blanket from around his shoulders and placed one end around Michael. The other end he draped around himself.

"Hold on to the blanket with one hand and place your free arm around my shoulder," Joe ordered as he helped Michael to his feet. "We've got to get out of here. Fast. I don't think the ceiling is going to last much longer."

Michael grunted and groaned as he moved to his feet, his lungs burning.

"Do you...think...we can make it?" he gasped, draping a weak arm around Joe's shoulder. "The fire! The smoke!"

"Father Michael, where's that faith you preach about all the time?" Joe said, frowning down at him. "Right now you've got to have enough for both of us. Do you understand?"

Michael nodded weakly, struggling to remain conscious. "We'll make it," he wheezed. "Let's go."

Joe drew the blanket up over his head and looked fearfully around him. For the first time in his life he actually felt threatened. The flames were quickly consuming the walls of the church, and the ceiling was creaking dangerously. It seemed as though the fire had consumed all of the air inside the church, and Joe strived to hold his short breaths for as long as he could.

"Hang on, Michael!" Joe shouted, half dragging Michael as he felt his feet step over the threshold.

Faye gasped as she watched Joe pull her brother from the smoky entrance. Weak with relief, she almost sank to her knees in thanks when suddenly her body stiffened. Shouts and screams rent the early morning air as the onlookers rushed to distance themselves from the blazing pyre. With a deafening crash, the tower collapsed onto the chapel, crushing the roof and toppling the east wall. Faye trembled and silently, reverently made the sign of the cross. God's house had been destroyed, but his faithful had been spared.

Breathing a deep, shuddering sigh of relief, Faye looked toward Joe and Michael. Joe was tending to Michael as though he were a close friend! As she watched Michael reach a hand to Joe's face, as though testing to see if he was all right, her heart swelled with love. Somehow more than one miracle had been performed tonight!

Faye rushed forward and fell to her knees beside Joe. The two men were black from the smoke, and their breaths came in between raspy coughs. Both were looking at her with red, smoke-filled eyes. She was torn between who she wanted to hug and kiss first.

Lunging into Joe's arms, Faye sobbed against his bare chest. *"Merci,"* she murmured, clinging hard to him.

After a minute that seemed to last a lifetime, she drew away from him and framed his face with her hands. "You could have been killed, yet you..."

Joe placed a forefinger to her lips. "Shh," he urged. "All is well. That's all that matters now."

Faye's eyes lingered for a moment longer on Joe, then she leaned over Michael where he still lay on the ground and hugged him to her. "Michael, Michael..." she whispered, rocking him in her arms. "You're all right. I thought you were dead."

Michael draped an arm around Faye's neck and kissed her softly on the cheek. "I owe a lot to Joe," he said hoarsely. "I would be dead if not for him."

"He's such a good man, Michael," Faye said, choking back a sob of joy. "I'm glad you see that now."

"I think I see many things I've been blind to," Michael said, easing Faye away from him as he moved to a sitting position.

Faye watched Michael peer over at Joe. Suddenly she realized that a crowd was forming close by. Soon the three of them would be surrounded. Uneasy, she looked back at her brother, once again afraid that the ugly differences between the two men would start yet another dreadful argument. Only this time they would have witnesses.

"Joe, come closer to me," Michael said, gesturing with a hand. "I've a few things that need saying."

Joe glanced from Faye to Michael, uneasy. Then, nodding, he moved on his knees closer and placed an arm possessively around Faye's waist.

Patting Joe on his back, his wrist limp, Michael smiled up at him. "I've made a few mistakes in my life," he said, coughing. "I intend to make up for them now that I have been given the chance."

Faye and Joe exchanged glances, then listened intently to Michael.

"Tonight proves to me that I must place more emphasis on ministering to the people in the way it was meant for me to," Michael said, again coughing. "I've brought danger to everyone at the mission by taking such a strong stand against the outlaws and encouraging vigilante activities."

Michael looked remorsefully toward his burning church. "I've a church to rebuild, and this time it must not be an ordinary one," he said, his voice stronger, more determined. "It will be one that will withstand fires and all evil that tries to penetrate its walls."

Joe clasped a hand on to Michael's shoulder. "And I'll be here working alongside everyone else to help build that church," he said thickly. "You can count on me."

Tears filled Faye's eyes, and she choked back a sob of joy, hardly believing what was happening before her very eyes. Her brother and the man she loved were making peace.

Then suddenly her heartbeat quickened when she remembered the child. Hurrying to her feet, she looked through the crowd and saw Celia clutching the baby, looking down at the child as though she and the infant girl were the only two people on the earth.

Faye placed a hand to her throat, touched by the gentle scene. Tears welled in her eyes when Gayland moved to Celia's side and placed an arm around her waist to also gaze down upon the little bundle.

"Faye?" Joe said, breaking into her thoughts. "Darling, I'm going to help Michael into the rectory. I think you'd best come along, also. We've something to tell him, don't we?"

Faye nodded toward Celia and Gayland. "Joe, would you look at them?" she said, drawing an audible breath of relief. "They've accepted the child without having even been asked. It's as though it *is* their child. Just look at the way they are looking at her. The little darling had a rough nine months before she was born, but think how blessed she will be the rest of her life."

Faye turned and leaned into Joe's arms. "Darling, everything is going to work out, isn't it?" she murmured. "Everything!"

"I'd say it's about time," Joe said easing her away. "Now let's help Michael into the rectory and have a serious talk about *us*. Though his church needs rebuilding, I don't want to put off our wedding another day."

"But without the church, where ... ?"

"The wedding ceremony can be performed in our home," he said, smiling down at her. "Yours and mine, Faye. We'll get the windows repaired and the mess cleaned up inside, and by evening tomorrow we can have quite a wedding celebration at our house."

"*Our* house?" Faye said, looking devotedly up at him. "Oh, how I love the sound of that!"

Then, as Michael rose onto wobbly legs, Faye supported him at one side, Joe at his other. Slowly they made their way toward the rectory.

Chapter Twenty-four

Faye stood at the mirror in her bedroom while Celia fussed over her, arranging her hair to hang neatly down her back. A chain of daisies formed a crown, and her hands idly smoothed the blue organdy material. The ruffled skirt edged in eyelet lace lay in three tiers, and the lacy petticoats peeped out from under the hem at her ankles.

"I've never seen such a lovely bride," Celia said, stepping aside to gaze at Faye. "Honey, if Joe doesn't burst with pride when he sees you, I'll be surprised."

Faye placed her hands to her hot cheeks. "Is it truly happening?" she asked, looking over at Celia. Her friend looked so beautiful and serene in her green gingham dress the color of her eyes. "Am I truly going to be married today? Does Joe truly want me to be his wife? For so long I doubted him."

Celia took Faye's hands from her face and held them fondly. "It's all real, hon," she murmured, smiling at her. "Everything! Your wedding. Your brother's approval.'' She swallowed hard. ''And the child that I can now call mine.''

Celia crept into Faye's arms and hugged her gently. ''Thank you, Faye,'' she murmured. ''From the very beginning you have been so dear. And now you have even managed to see that at long last Gayland and I are parents. Oh, how lucky we all are!''

''Oui,'' Faye said softly, ''we have been lucky.'' At her quiet statement, a shiver ran through her. Thinking over the events of the past year, never would she have dreamed she could be so happy.

Celia stepped back from Faye, her gaze troubled. ''What's the matter, hon?'' she asked, placing a hand to Faye's brow. ''Are you coming down with something? You just shivered as though you'd caught the chill.''

Laughing nervously, Faye swung away from Celia and went to the window to look toward the beckoning forest. ''I'm all right,'' she murmured. ''It's just that so much has happened to me since I left New Orleans. I had so dreaded coming here, but now I could never be happy anywhere else. Joe is my life— my every heartbeat.'' She clasped her hands together before her and spun around to face Celia again. ''Oh, Celia, I am so very, very happy!''

Celia lifted a fringed shawl from a chair and went and placed it around Faye's shoulders. ''Then let us be on our way,'' she said softly. ''I think the men have had enough time today to repair the cabin—except for the windowpanes that were shot out. For a while buckskin will have to do. I'm sure the women have been cooking since daybreak. A feast has been planned for after the wedding.''

''And Michael is probably pacing the floor in the study like a nervous husband waiting for his wife to give birth,'' Faye said, giggling softly. Then her smile faded. ''That he is going to be a part of this wedding at all is a miracle. Indeed it is a miracle that Michael and Joe are even speaking decently to each other.''

''Well, let's say amen to all these recent miracles,'' Celia said, laughing softly. She placed a hand to Faye's elbow and began guiding her toward the door. ''My little miracle is sound asleep just down the hall. Little Annetta is in safe enough hands with the wet nurse. Father Michael chose the most competent of women to look after her.''

Faye turned with teary eyes to Celia, happiness bubbling over inside her. She lunged into her friend's arms and hugged her. ''Celia, you finally have what you so dearly have wanted for so long,'' she cried softly. ''And so do I. Isn't it wonderful?''

Celia sighed. ''Very,'' she whispered, caressing Faye's back. ''Very.''

Faye clung to the seat of the buggy between Michael and Celia as they drew closer to the merriment just ahead. Laughter rang in the air, then everyone drew quiet and the banjo player and fiddler ceased to play as the crowd stepped aside so that Michael could guide the buggy toward the hitching post.

Faye's eyes searched for Joe, and she found him among the crowd, so handsome in a new buckskin outfit that her insides melted with passion. Straightening her back, she continued to gaze at him while Michael climbed from the seat and secured the horse's reins and helped Celia and then Faye from the buggy.

As though in a trance, Faye stood as Joe walked square-shouldered toward her, his dark, fathomless eyes proud and sure. His breeches were close-fitting and showed the play of his muscles in his lean thighs with each stride. His face, bronzed from the sun, shone from a fresh shave. His long, dark hair hung loose and free to his shoulders. Open at the throat, his buckskin shirt revealed his thick frond of dark chest hair, and he wore new beaded moccasins.

Radiantly happy, Faye smiled up at him as he stopped before her and offered her his arm. Michael held his Bible, ready to walk behind them, and Gayland tore himself away from the settlers who had been eagerly working since daybreak to ready the cabin and came to escort Celia beside Father Michael.

"May I have the honor, beautiful lady?" Joe said huskily as Faye slipped her hand through his arm. "Are you ready to become my wife?"

"Oui," Faye said, looking devotedly up at him. "I am ready." For a moment she rested her forehead against him. "I'm so happy, Joe."

Then realizing that all eyes were on them, Faye pulled away and walked with him, arm in arm, toward the cabin, their cabin. Everyone stepped aside, making a narrow path for them to walk along.

Faye's eyes widened in wonder, and she stopped in midstep when she saw a small mound of rubble blocking the door of the cabin. "My word, what is that?" she gasped, studying the debris spread across the ground in front of the door. "Joe, what on earth *is* it?"

Stifling a laugh behind his hand, Joe gave Bart an amused glance. "It seems my friend, the humorous one, is having some fun at our expense," he said, chuckling along with the rest of the onlookers. "It's a tradition here in the Ozarks for the groom's best friend to delay the ceremony so that everyone can have a good laugh."

Faye looked up at Joe and then once again at the pile of trees and grapevines that blocked the path over which the wedding party must travel. She glanced over at Bart and saw the wicked smile and dancing eyes and could not help but be amused. She tried to stifle a laugh, but failed miserably.

"Bart, shame on you," Faye scolded playfully as Bart and several other men hurried to remove the debris. "You just wait until you decide to get married. Joe and I will torment you forever!"

"Find me someone just like you and I'll get married in an instant," Bart teased back, winking at Faye. "Until then I think ol' Bart will continue playin' the field."

"I'll let you know tomorrow whether or not you're right to do that," Joe said, giving Faye a teasing glance. "Perhaps I'll give Faye to you if she doesn't work out. What do you say to that, Bart?"

Faye looked quickly up at Joe, then smiled sweetly when she saw the twinkle in his eyes. "Darling," she said in a low purr, "perhaps it will be I who will be on the lookout for a new man if you don't fill the bill. There are many available soldiers at Fort Smith. Just you remember that."

Loud laughter and applause from all sides made her face turn crimson. She cleared her throat and looked straight ahead, relieved that the door was no longer blocked. She had had enough of the teasing and tormenting.

Her fingers trembling, her heart pounding, Faye proceeded up the path to the cabin and stepped inside with Joe as Bart opened the door for them. At the sight, she found it impossible to so much as breathe. In a matter of hours the cabin had been transformed into something lovely and breathtaking! No longer did she see handmade furniture. While she had been resting earlier in the day, several pieces of furniture had been taken from the rectory and brought to the cabin. Long, tapered candles burned brightly on cherrywood tables, lighting the room that smelled sweetly of roses and all other assorted flowers in vases positioned around the room.

A plush upholstered sofa sat before the fireplace with matching chairs on each side. A dining room table crafted from solid maple was piled high with gifts. A large, ornately framed mirror over a dresser reflected a beautiful canopy bed with a feather-filled comforter draped across it.

Windowpanes that had been purchased for another settler and had just arrived the previous day had been given to Joe for his new bride. They were covered now by lemon satin curtains that hung down to a thick Brussels carpet on the floor.

Faye was breathless as she turned and eyed Joe with wonder. "Joe? You did all of this for me?" she murmured, close to tears. "Why, *c'est magnifique!*"

Joe leaned down close to her face. "Darling, the outlaws did us a favor last night," he said softly. "When they tore the hell out of this place, it gave me cause to take a second look at it. It was not a proper place to bring a bride, now was it?"

"I hadn't complained," Faye said, sniffling back a sob of joy.

"But you do approve?"

"*Oui*, totally."

"Then what are we waiting for? Let's have ourselves a wedding."

Faye stepped to Joe's side and waited for as many people as possible to squeeze into the cabin. When

Celia brought Faye a bridal bouquet of lilies of the valley and pink roses and placed them in her trembling hands, Faye could not help but let a tear escape from the corner of her eye.

Holding her chin high, Faye then looked with love at Michael as he came and stood facing her and Joe in his black robe. His blue eyes misted as he looked into hers. She swallowed back a growing lump in her throat as Joe circled his arm through hers and took her hand.

"In the name of the Father..." Michael began.

The celebration was over and the stars were flickering in the night sky. As Faye and Joe stood arm in arm watching the last buggy amble down the path into the forest, Faye trembled as a cool breeze lifted her hair from her bare shoulders.

Joe looked down at her, questioning her with his eyes, then in one sweep he had her up in his arms and was walking her across the threshold of their cabin. "My darling, I've waited long enough," he said huskily, smiling down at her as she laughed softly, her cheeks rosy, her eyes as blue as the early sky of spring. "It was pure hell having to dance and eat while all along I just wanted everyone to leave so that we could be alone as man and wife."

"And now we are alone," Faye said, clinging to his neck. "Kind sir, what do you have planned for me? Is it something that will make me remember my wedding night forever?"

Joe kicked the door shut with his foot and walked toward the bed. He chuckled lowly. "I guess I have much to prove to you, don't I?"

"Well, yes, I hope so," Faye said as he placed her gently on the bed. "Just where shall you start, love? Surely you no longer find me a challenge since I am now merely your wife."

Lifting the crown of daisies from Faye's head, Joe placed them gently on the nightstand. "Merely my wife?" he said, chuckling. "Darling, it is almost incomprehensible that you are. Only a week ago I would have laughed at anyone who would have predicted that we would be married. I thought you still looked on me as insufferable...arrogant. I'm so glad that you have placed those feelings behind you. My reasons for behaving so..."

Faye turned to Joe and placed a finger to his lips. "Let's not speak of the past ever again," she murmured. "Of feelings...of anything. We have now and all tomorrows. That's all that is important, Joe."

She ran her tongue seductively over his lower lip. "Love me, darling," she whispered, her sure fingers slowly lifting the hem of his buckskin shirt. "Tonight is the beginning of our tomorrows."

Joe lifted his arms and let her fully remove the shirt. His breath caught as she splayed her fingers over his chest and lowered her mouth to one of his nipples to nip it with her teeth.

"Enough of that," he said, laughing throatily. He rose from the bed then and undressed while candles burned low and the flames on the hearth cast their weaving, dancing shadows on the walls and ceiling.

Faye moved from the bed and stood beside him. She, too, began undressing, slowly and seductively as he watched her, his dark eyes branding her.

Both nude, they looked into each other's eyes and smiled unspoken words to each other, then crept back onto the bed. Joe knelt down over Faye, his lips and tongue setting her afire as he started worshiping her body, beginning at the hollow of her throat, then moving to her breasts, then crossing her abdomen.

Breathless with desire, Faye urged him back up so that their lips could meet in a fiery kiss. Her hands clung to his sinewed shoulders as he plunged his hardness deep within her and began his eager strokes, causing her to become wild and weak with building need.

She arched her hips and met his thrusts, moving with him, taking from him as she was giving. With a fierceness he held her close, his tongue surging between her parted lips, stirring her to frenzied passion.

With a moan of ecstasy she clung to him, consumed by his demanding needs, which matched her own. His kiss deepened. His hands molded her breasts, then traveled hotly across her abdomen, then lower, touching and caressing the core of her womanhood while he continued his strokes within her.

Pleasure and pain fused within Faye into something sweet as Joe thrust harder than ever before during their lovemaking. She inhaled shakily and closed her eyes, his lips now on her breast, flicking his tongue around its nipple. Her entire being throbbed with building ecstasy. It was near to exploding, and then, abruptly, he pulled away from her, leaving her wondering as she looked up at him.

Joe leaned over her, smiling devilishly down at her. "Did you like the beginning?" he teased, his hands kneading her breasts. "Shall I continue?"

Breathless, tingling from head to toe, Faye smiled seductively up at him. "And if I said no?" she whispered, smoothing her fingers over his dampened chest. "What would you do?"

Looking down, she stroked his full hardness, glad that it made him suck in his breath with agony. "Darling, I do believe you would suffer more than I," she said, laughing throatily.

He grabbed her hand, pinning it down on the mattress, as his eyes burned into her. "You know me so well," he said, chuckling. "Shall we continue?"

"Please do," Faye beckoned, scarcely recognizing her voice, it was so husky and deep.

Again he impaled her with his hardness. He scorched her lips with a heated kiss while their bodies strained hungrily together. Desire shot through Faye as she felt herself climbing to heights of wondrous bliss. His warmth inside her was spreading, a familiar surge of heat that momentarily robbed her of all feeling except that of intense pleasure.

She rocked with Joe as she felt his body quake and quiver.

And when it was over, they lay there, clinging, kissing....

"Well, hello, Mrs. Harrison," Joe said, twining his fingers through her hair, drawing her lips close. "I like the sound of that. Do you?"

"Nothing has ever sounded as sweet," Faye said, sighing. She flicked her tongue across his bottom lip. "Nor has anything ever tasted as sweet. Darling, how I do love you."

"The wedding was nice, wasn't it, Faye?" Joe said, easing away from her to lie on his side and look around him. "And by damn if my cabin doesn't look a sight better!"

Faye laughed softly and snuggled against him. "The wedding was beautiful," she murmured. "And your...our...cabin is beautiful."

Joe framed her face between his hands. "Nothing is as beautiful as you," he said, his voice low. "Nothing."

A loud knock on the door drew him away from Faye. In one swift movement he bolted from the bed and drew on his breeches, throwing the feather-filled comforter over Faye. "Who the hell could be here tonight?" he growled.

Stomping to the door, Joe opened it with a yank, then took a step backward when Bart stormed on in, his face flushed anxiously. Bart gave Faye a nervous, apologetic glance, then stood firmly before Joe.

"Joe, excuse the interruption, but I think you'd best get dressed fast," he said hoarsely. "Dammit all to hell, Joe, while everyone was here at the wedding, almost nearly all of their homes were ransacked and their horses stolen." He doubled a fist at his side. "This is the last straw, Joe. We've got to hunt the thieves down this time until we find every last one of them. Everyone is asking for your help, Joe. No one knows the art of tracking better than you."

Bart looked nervously over at Faye. "Sorry, ma'am," he murmured. "But this can't be helped. Joe is needed. I'm sure you understand."

Faye held the comforter close beneath her chin, eyeing Joe warily. "Joe?" she asked, her voice thin. "Joe, what are you going to do?"

"Faye, I have no choice," Joe said, giving her a lingering look, then going to his gun belt and swinging it around his waist. In one fast sweep he had his shirt over his head and his feet fitted into his moccasins.

Grabbing his rifle, he went to Faye and leaned down over her. "Honey, please understand," he said softly. "This is a part of what marrying me will be about. When I'm called up, I must go. I'm needed, sweetheart. Tell me you understand."

A shiver coursed along Faye at the thought of anything happening to him after she had just won him.

But she must be strong, she must stand behind him,

"How long will you be gone?" she asked, placing a steady hand to his cheek.

"For as long as it takes to find the sons of bitches," Joe growled, then blushed and lowered his eyes. "Sorry. I've got to learn to watch my language now that I've got me a pretty wife."

Faye laughed softly. "Darling, go on and do what you must," she said, kissing him on the cheek. "I'll be here waiting when you return. But please be very careful. I couldn't bear it if anything happened to you."

"No outlaw is going to make you a widow," Joe reassured her, squaring his shoulders as he rose to his full height. "But I'll make a few outlaws' wives wish they had chosen different husbands. I hope we can chase down all the dirty thieves and get them behind bars before any more decent folk have to suffer."

Joe gave Faye the rifle. "Use this if you are ever threatened in my absence," he said somberly. "You'll have to learn how to protect yourself because I will be gone sometimes for lengthy spells."

"I think I can handle that," Faye said, her eyes wide. She laid the rifle aside and leaned up on an elbow as Joe rushed to the door. She smiled reassuringly at his last lingering look.

Then, dispirited, Faye crept from the bed and drew on a robe. Barefoot, she went to the door and twisted the crude lock. Her eyes landed on the crown of daisies, now sadly wilted.

Going to stand before the warmth of the fire, she began plucking the petals from the flowers and making a wish on each, trying to forget the sound of the horses as they had ridden away.

Softly, she cursed the dread that had formed a pit in her stomach, cursed the outlaws...and cursed Joe Harrison.

She had asked Joe if he was going to make this a wedding night she would remember forever. Settling down onto the plush sofa before the fire, she laughed to herself. "I do believe you did, Joe Harrison. I do believe you did."

Chapter Twenty-five

Raindrops pelted the roof overhead and loud claps of thunder reverberated through the forest. Faye felt the cabin's floor shake under her feet. Momentarily pausing with her candlemaking, she stole occasional glances toward the window where her curtains were drawn shut so that she could not see the lurid flashes of lightning in the distant sky. Would she ever get over her fear of storms? And Joe was out in the storm this very moment, perhaps in hand-to-hand combat with an outlaw. She closed her eyes and shivered at the thought.

"The storm will soon pass," Celia reassured her, bending over the bed to wrap a blanket more snugly around Annetta. "As will our husbands return soon. Nothing will happen to them, Faye. Please keep thinking that."

Faye tried to concentrate on the task at hand, the fire on the hearth warm against her back. She smoothed a fallen lock of hair from her brow and stepped closer to her dining table, then slipped another wick made from the silky down of the milk-weed plant over a candle rod and dipped it in melted tallow.

"They've been gone for almost a week now," she murmured, watching the tallow as it began to harden. "Why are they gone so long, Celia? Surely something terrible must have happened. I can't shake off the feeling of dread that follows me around like the plague!" She glared at the window, her jaw tight. "And now this dreaded storm? It's almost too much to bear."

Celia walked to the table and arranged a wick over a candle rod and began dipping it along with Faye. "Honey, this is just the beginning, you know," she said softly, her green eyes golden as they picked up the glow of the fire. "This is just a part of being a wife in the wilderness. Don't get discouraged now or your marriage is doomed. You don't want that, do you?"

Faye knew that what Celia said was true. When Joe returned, he could not find her filled with dread and doubts. She must prove to him that she was strong and willing to accept these times that he would be gone from her.

"I'll be all right," she said, lifting the dripping candle from the tallow. Tying the wick onto a long stick from which other candles were hanging, she walked away from the chore at hand and bent over the bed to gaze down at the sleeping bundle of joy. "And you, Celia. Don't you worry about Gayland.

He'll return unharmed, also. He doesn't have only you to guide him back, but also his daughter. He has been twice blessed.''

Celia tied her hardening candle and moved to Faye's side, peering at the pink face framed with dark, thick hair. "I didn't think Gayland would join Bart and Joe," she said softly. "But after seeing the destruction and realizing just how many horses were stolen, he saw no choice but to do his part."

"I admire him," Faye said, turning to Celia to take her hands. "The soldiers didn't have to ask more than once for him to join them. He's a brave man, Celia."

"Along with countless other husbands," Celia said, smiling weakly. "But I wonder if Gayland can keep up with the young ones?"

Faye laughed gently, her blue eyes twinkling. "Celia, a man is only as old as he acts," she said. "The child has made Gayland feel like a man of twenty. He'll be all right."

"Joe promised that he would be," Celia murmured. "So, yes, he will be."

"You put a lot of faith in Joe Harrison, don't you?"

"All my faith. All of it."

"Everyone depends on him so much."

"He is a dependable man. And he's your husband, Faye. How proud you must be."

Faye hugged Celia. "I am sure no more proud than you are of your husband," she declared softly.

She stepped away and went to a large kettle that had already been placed over the fire. "Shall we, Celia?" she asked, giving her a glance over her shoulder. "Are you ready to pinch your nose?"

"I guess I'm as ready as I'll ever be," Celia said, laughing softly. She looked down at her baby. "Poor Annetta. She will have to tolerate the smell because she won't know how to cover her nose."

Reaching for the blanket, she placed a corner over Annetta's nose and giggled. "There, that ought to do it," she whispered, then turned and walked toward the fire. "You have enough ashes for several bars of soap. Every spring enough soap should be made to last a year. Next April we'll make soap in a mass quantity outside where it won't be so messy."

"Or stinky!" Faye giggled, standing over a barrel, pouring water over ashes that Joe had saved from the fireplace, having expected to make the soap himself.

Faye watched the water trickle out through a hole near the bottom of the barrel and into a bucket placed beneath it. This brown liquid was the lye used in making the soap.

She then took the bucket of lye water and placed it in the large kettle that hung over the fire, along with fats and grease that Joe had saved from cooking and butchering. This mixture was left to cook slowly until it thickened to form a soft, jellylike yellow soap.

"Let's sit down and rest before the fire while the mixture is cooking," Celia said, pouring two cups of coffee. "It's been a long day. It can be an even longer night."

Faye settled down on the sofa and accepted a cup from Celia as her friend sat down beside her. "I'm glad Michael brought you and Annetta out here today," she murmured, sipping on the coffee. "I guess he knew that I was just about at my wits' end with worry."

"No, he knew that you needed help making candles and soap," Celia said, laughing softly.

Faye looked over at Celia, her eyes wide. "Yes, my brother knows me so well," she said, laughing along with her. "And so do you. It's as though we've known each other forever, Celia. I feel as close to you as sisters must surely feel. I hope you feel the same."

Celia picked up her embroidery that she had brought with her. "I have felt a stronger bond than that," she said, drawing the needle through the fabric. "I have felt motherly toward you more than sisterly."

She glanced over at Faye. "But I never wanted you to think that I was trying to take the place of your mother," she added. "Perhaps it's best if we do behave more like sisters."

"*Oui*, perhaps," Faye said. In her mind's eye she could see her mother, and the longing for her was becoming less in her heart as time was passing. She had begun to accept the loss.

Celia cleared her throat nervously. "Gayland says that the low-hanging hornets' nests and busy woodpeckers are signs of an approaching severe winter," she said, taking another stitch. "But of course it's just superstitions that he pays close attention to. You know, the same as he has said that the crackling of the burning back log in a fire foretells a coming storm."

The back log in the fireplace crackled and sizzled, causing a strained silence between Celia and Faye. Then they burst out laughing as they looked at each other.

"It seems that superstition is a bit late," Faye said. "It's already raining cats and dogs outside."

Then Faye's laughter and smile faded when she recalled that Gayland had foretold his own illness.

"Superstitions are all utter hogwash, you know," Celia said, noting Faye's sudden silence. She placed her embroidery aside and rose to her feet and went to the table. "Let's see how the candles are doing."

Faye rose, understanding Celia's wanting to change the subject. She twitched her nose at the smell of the lye soap. "I don't think we have to check on the soap," she said, flipping the skirt of her dress around as she went to the table to softly touch the hardening candles. "I don't want to get any closer to that stuff than I have to. Before it's over it might run us out of the cabin into the rain."

Suddenly Faye's hand dropped to her side. Her eyes wide with alarm, she silently questioned Celia.

"Yes, I heard a horse's snort, also," Celia whispered, moving cautiously toward the window. "But I didn't hear anyone ride up."

"The muddy ground would muffle the horse's approach," Faye whispered back, hurrying to grab the rifle. She primed and loaded it, then positioned herself before the door, breathing hard. "What if it is a stray outlaw? Oh, Celia, I don't want to shoot anyone!"

Celia's fingers trembled as she inched them toward the curtain. "Faye, did you ever consider that it might be Joe?" she asked, giving Faye a quick glance. "Perhaps he's finally returned!"

"I can't take the chance that it's not," Faye said, steadying the rifle, aiming for the door. "Joe's been gone so long. Perhaps the outlaws have discovered that I am here without his protection. They might even be planning to . . . to . . . rape me."

"Faye, stop that!" Celia scolded. "Remember what I said earlier? You've got to remember that being alone goes with being a wife in the wilderness, and you mustn't let your mind conjure up all sorts of wild things while you're alone. You could go mad in the process. Now let me take a look at who it is. We both may be pleasantly surprised."

Suddenly the door swung open, startling Faye so much that she pulled the trigger. The gun jerked violently in her hand, throwing her backward. She fell clumsily to the floor, looking up at the ceiling where the explosion of the ball had torn a hole in a wooden beam.

"Dammit, Faye!" Joe growled, storming on into the room, soaking wet. He towered over her as she lay there, looking up at him, stunned. "This is the second time you've taken a shot at me." He leaned down and jerked the rifle away from her. "Wasn't once enough?"

"Joe?" Faye said weakly, her eyes riveted to his wet, angry face. "Oh, Joe. I didn't know..."

"Yes, that's apparent," he said, tossing the rifle aside. Annetta's crying drew his attention away from Faye, softening his mood. He looked toward the bed, seeing the baby's arms waving wildly in the air as Celia rushed to her.

Faye rose, looking apologetically toward Celia. "I'm so sorry," she murmured. "I didn't mean to frighten Annetta."

Then she turned back around and found Joe looking down at her with a soft smile. She smiled weakly at him, then lunged into his arms, pressing her face into his wet buckskin shirt as she hugged him fiercely. "Darling, you're home," she cried, reveling in his closeness as he drew her more snugly into his embrace. "I so feared for your safety! And...you're...home."

"It's a homecoming I'll never forget," he said, chuckling. He gave Gayland a look over Faye's shoulder as he stepped into the room, dripping from head to toe. "Nor will Gayland. I doubt if he'll ever trust opening our front door again. Here we have been out for days chasing down outlaws only to be shot at by my own wife." He laughed loudly. "The outlaws would have a good horse laugh over that."

Celia's eyes lit up, and tears filled her eyes when she saw Gayland moving toward her. Tears ran down her cheeks as he enveloped both her and the child in one embrace. "Oh, Gayland," she cried. "Gayland."

Joe eased Faye from his arms and looked down at her, his eyes hauntingly dark. "I didn't mean to scold you so severely, darling," he apologized. "But please check the next time before firing. I'll be coming and going all the time. I don't want to worry about being shot every time I return to my home."

"I think I've learned my lesson," Faye said, laughing softly. "It won't happen again."

Joe sniffed and looked around him. "What is that ungodly smell?" he asked. Then he spied the large pot hanging over the flames. "Ah, yes, soap. So you've not been idle." He looked toward the table and saw the candles hanging in a long line, then down at Faye. "You have become quite the little homemaker, have you?" he said softly. "All domesticated and beautiful at the same time?"

"I'm trying," Faye said, smiling up at him. "And you? How did things go for you?"

Joe glanced over at Gayland. "Tell 'em, Gayland," he said, his eyes dancing.

Gayland placed an arm around Celia's waist. He looked at his wife and child, then smiled smugly from Faye to Joe. "Well, it's like this," he said, his chest swelling with pride. "I rode side by side with Joe and chased those outlaws clean across the countryside until we captured them."

"All of them?" Faye gasped, her eyes wide.

Joe took her hand and pulled it around his lean torso. "That's virtually impossible," he said thickly. "But we've got enough of them imprisoned at the fort to keep things quiet for a while. We also rounded up most of the stolen horses."

"So it was successful enough?" Faye questioned, glad that it was over, no matter how successful! For a while she had her husband with her again. She would cherish this time moment by moment.

"For now it is," Joe said, winking at Gayland. "Now, Gayland, I think we both need time alone with our wives, don't you?"

Gayland glanced down at Celia. "Honey, I've brought a buggy so you and the baby wouldn't have to travel in the rain," he said softly. "Thanks for leaving a note on the table, telling me where you were. Joe had stopped by to get out of the rain for a moment before traveling on here. It made us both feel better to know that you and Faye were weathering the storm together."

"I believe we'll be doing this quite often in the future," Celia said, reaching to pat Faye on the cheek. "That's what friends are for."

Faye smiled over at Celia and nodded, feeling so very pleased. Everything in life seemed to be working out for her.

At long last, life was wonderfully sweet.

Chapter Twenty-six

Oaks glowed like hot coals in the forest, and on the high plateaus broom sedge grew coppery in the setting autumn sun. Along the banks of the creeks and rivers, sycamores had raised their bare white arms in surrender to winter's advance.

It had been another full day of socializing as the settlement took full advantage of the Indian summer. Everyone had gathered together to enjoy a nutting party, a log rolling and a taffy pull.

But the forest no longer rang with laughter or the squawk of the fiddle. It was now quiet except for the squirrels scampering along limbs, their jaws puffed with acorns.

Faye and Joe walked arm in arm in the twilight. "I'm not sure which is the loveliest in the Ozarks, spring or fall," Joe said, his gaze taking in the autumn hues. "Don't the colors of the leaves just blind you with their brilliance?"

"I doubt if autumn can be as beautiful anywhere else as in the Ozarks," Faye said, trembling slightly in the chill wind.

Joe drew her shawl more snugly around her shoulders, and together they began to move back in the direction of the cabin. "Enjoy it now, for all signs point to a long, cold winter. All the woolly worms I've seen are dark and have a thick coat of hair."

Faye moved away from him and swung around to stand in his path. "Darling, please don't tell me that you're superstitious, also," she said, her eyes twinkling. "First Gayland, then Celia, and now *you*?"

"Superstitious?" Joe said, swinging her back around to his side to resume walking through the woods. "Darling, what I said about the woolly worms is pure fact."

"All right," Faye acquiesced, giggling. "It's pure fact." She then looked quickly up at him. "Darling, I had a wonderful time today," she said with a contented sigh. "But I must say that the taffy pull has left me sore."

"Sore muscles never hurt anyone," Joe said with a chuckle. "It's good for a person."

"Joe, wasn't annetta sweet today?" Faye said, changing the subject. "She's already forming a personality. I just love being around her."

Joe drew Faye around and into his arms. He gazed down at her with intense, dark eyes, his jaw set. "What do you say we go home and make ourselves our own baby?'' he said hoarsely. ''Then Annetta could have herself a little playmate.'' He chuckled low. ''And, my dear, so could *you*.''

A gentle passion warmed Faye's heart as she looked adoringly up at him. ''Is this what you want?'' she murmured. ''A child?''

''Now that I have you,'' he said, kissing her brow, ''I'd like a daughter or son, or possibly both, to complete our little paradise right here on earth. What do you say? Shall we?''

''Oh, *oui*,'' Faye murmured, melting into his arms. ''That would be so wonderful.''

At Joe's quick intake of breath, she eased herself away from him. Following his gaze, she gasped when she saw what had drawn his undivided attention. A great herd of buffalo was wandering across a high plateau beyond the forest. As far as the eye could see stood hundreds and hundreds of the native beasts.

''Now that the outlaws have been thinned out, the buffalo may have a chance to breed again,'' Joe said in awe.

They watched for a moment, then moved on to their cabin. Once inside, Joe removed Faye's shawl and drew her into his embrace. ''Any regrets?'' he asked, his eyes dark and haunting. ''Do you still miss New Orleans?''

For a moment Faye's thoughts were filled with fancy gowns, sweet-smelling corsages, laughter-filled ballrooms and young men bowing low as they asked for a dance.

"Do I?" she said, cocking her head to pretend that she had to search hard for the answer.

Then she laughed and began leading Joe to their bed. "Darling, no," she murmured. "I don't miss New Orleans. How could I when there is *you*? You are now my hopes, my dreams, my *pleasure*. Everything and everyone else seems so trivial in comparison."

"That's what I wanted to hear," Joe said huskily, lying down with her on the bed. He cradled her close and kissed her with lazy familiarity.

Within his arms, Faye had found a sweet contentment. All the hardships of the past year had led up to this moment. And for this great reward, she would not have changed a thing.

* * * * *

COMING NEXT MONTH

#19 RIDES A HERO—Heather Graham Pozzessere

Shannon McCahy despised the cruel Civil War that had robbed her of all but her precious land. Though the conflict was over, a new breed of ruthless men had descended upon the Missouri border to threaten her loved ones. But only the fugitive Rebel Malachi Slater would shatter her defenses and claim the beautiful Yankee's heart as they joined forces in a desperate rescue mission.

#20 SAMARA—Patricia Potter

As war threatened the uneasy peace between England and America in 1812, fiery Samara O'Neill would not sit idle. But when she rashly hid herself aboard her brother's schooner, she hadn't counted on being taken prisoner by dangerous British privateer Reese Hampton. Within her reckless heart Samara had never imagined her greatest adventure would be loving Reese.